COMMAND

— BOOK 7 IN THE STORM MC SERIES —

NINA LEVINE

This is a work of fiction. Names, characters, places, and incidents are a
product of the author's imagination. Locales and public names are
sometimes used for atmospheric purposes. Any resemblance to actual
people, living or dead, or to businesses, companies, events, institutions,
or locales is completely coincidental.

Editing by Karen Louise Rohde Faergemann at The Word Wench
Editing Services
Cover Design ©2015 by Romantic Book Affair Designs
Cover Photography by Eric Battershell
Models Jelena Abbou & Billy Cluver

Dedication

This book is dedicated to my readers.

You opened your hearts to my words two years ago and you will never know what that means to me.
Before I published my first book, I was going through my own storm. Storms can vary in their intensity, and some have the power to devastate you. But, sometimes you survive the devastation, and you find the beauty in the journey.

Sometimes there's a blessing in the storm.

Chapter One
Scott

Decisions.

We're free to make them, but never free from living with their consequences.

I sat on my bike outside my house, contemplating the future. The path ahead appeared clear to me, but even so, the doubts swirled and my gut churned with concern. One wrong step and the consequences could cause everything Storm had worked for over the years to come crashing down. Losing seven men today had been a kick in the gut, but the club would be stronger without them.

We had a lot of rebuilding to do, but I believed our club could achieve anything it set out to do, so long as we treaded carefully.

"Scott."

Turning, I eyed Harlow as she made her way down the front steps and walked towards me.

Jesus, can she get any more beautiful?

My gaze traced her curves. I took in the skimpy denim shorts she wore with the frayed edges that barely covered her ass, and the tiny, white tank she had stretched across her chest, giving me an eyeful of one of my favourite views in the world. Her tanned skin glowed as if she'd spent the day in the sun, but I doubted that, as her mum's café was too busy at the moment for her to take a day off during the week.

"Hey, you," she greeted me with a smile as she looped her arms around my neck and kissed me.

Fuck, having her arms around me, and her lips on mine, would never get old. The last few months had been hard while she'd pulled away. But since I'd managed to break through to her at Christmas, she'd been finding her way back to me.

I slid an arm around her waist and pulled her closer. As she ended the kiss, I cocked my head to the side and said, "You changed your hair."

She flicked her hair with her hand. "Yeah, do you like it? I'm not sure if I like it brown."

While I preferred her blonde, she could dye her hair

8

fucking purple and I'd still love it. "It looks good, baby."

Her eyes searched mine and she frowned. "You don't seem your usual self this afternoon. What's wrong?"

I moved off the bike and raked my hand through my hair. Burdening Harlow with club business was the last thing I wanted to do; she had enough other shit to deal with at the moment. "Just club shit going on. Nothing for you to worry about."

Her eyes narrowed at me. "Bullshit, Scott. Tell me the truth." Fuck, she hadn't spoken to me in that way for far too long. I'd almost forgotten how much I liked it.

I raised my brows. "Been awhile since I've seen this side of you, sweetheart. You wanna keep that up and I'll show you what I like to do with dirty mouths." My cock was so damn hard for her. From the minute I woke up to the goddamn minute I slept at night, I fucking wanted her. Our sex life hadn't fully recovered since Christmas – she still held something back from me, and as much as I'd tried to figure out how to fix it, I'd come up empty.

Her breathing stilled and she bit her lip before it spread into a sexy smile. She pressed her body against mine and placed her hands on my chest, and fuck if that didn't shoot a whole new level of need straight to my dick. "You should show me." Her voice was all breathy and her eyes sparkled with desire. "But not until you tell me what's going on."

Jesus.

My woman stood in front of me, demanding to know

stuff she hadn't been interested in for too long, and as much as I wanted to unload and have her involved in my life again, I *needed* to fuck her. Harlow was more turned on than I'd seen her in a long fucking time - no way was I passing up this opportunity.

Decisions.

It all came back to priorities.

I slid my arm around her so I could take hold of her ass. Bending my face to hers, I growled, "How about you get your sexy ass upstairs and I'll show you how much trouble a dirty mouth can get you in. And then if you're not completely worn out, we'll talk."

Her eyes didn't leave mine, and she nodded her agreement. She didn't say anything, but no words were needed.

I let her go and jerked my chin towards the stairs. "I want you in the shower, baby. Naked."

She didn't hesitate and a moment later, I tracked her ass as she made her way upstairs. Fuck, a man could spend hours watching that ass.

I followed her inside but made a stop in the kitchen on the way to the shower so I could fill the fridge with the beer I'd brought home. The sight that greeted me in the kitchen caused my steps to falter. "Harlow!" I called out. "Kitchen, now."

Fuck the shower; I wanted her on the fucking kitchen counter.

A minute later she appeared in the kitchen.

10

Naked.

Frowning at me, she asked, "What's wrong?"

My eyes dropped to her chest before moving back up to hold her gaze. "Nothing's wrong. In fact, I'd say something is very right." I gestured at the counter where she had yet to clean her mess up from baking. The minute I'd eyed the cream cheese wrapper, the white chocolate packet and the red food colouring, I knew what she'd been making. "Been a long time since you've made red velvet cake, baby."

She smiled and took a step closer to me. "Been a long time since I've seen your eyes crinkle like that," she murmured.

Fuck, those words were the best ones I'd heard all day.

I closed the distance between us. "Red velvet cake means more than just baking."

"What do you mean?" Her forehead pulled together as she thought about that. I was surprised she didn't know.

"There are two reasons you bake red velvet – either you've had a good day or I've done something to make you happy. Seeing as though I've done nothing, I'm guessing you've had a good day, and that makes me fuckin' happy because, like I said, it's been too long since you've baked red velvet cake."

She placed one of her hands on my chest. "You make me happier than you realise, Scott. I'm sorry I don't show you that enough."

I curled my hand around her neck and pulled her face

close to mine. "You don't ever apologise for something you had no control over in the first place. I see you working like fuck to get yourself through this and that's enough for me." Sliding my free hand over her naked ass, I pulled her body tight against mine, and dropped my lips to hers to claim the kiss I'd been aching for all day. When I was done with her lips, I angled my face away from hers enough so I could appreciate her curves again. "Fuck, Harlow, I wanna hear about your day, but I can't wait another minute to get inside you."

She gave me one of her sexy-as-fuck smiles and moved her hands to undo my jeans. "I can't wait, either."

Those four words were all it took for me to finally lose the last shreds of self-control I'd been holding onto. While she removed my jeans and boxers, I pulled my cut and t-shirt off. When we were both naked, I lifted her by the ass and sat her on the kitchen counter. She wrapped her arms and legs around me, and I sucked in a breath at how damn good that felt.

"You ready to fly?" I asked as I ran my hands over her skin.

"I'm always ready to fly with you." Her voice had turned all husky and sexy, and fuck if the words she spoke didn't continue to turn me on. Something had definitely changed in her today and after I made her come, I would be getting to the bottom of what it was. I needed to make sure it stayed that way; seeing her happy was my number one priority. And hell, my dick needed to make sure it stayed that way, too.

Taking hold of her, I ran my dick through her wetness, and growled, "I need hard today. You good with that?"

Her lips smashed down onto mine and she surprised the hell out of me with a demanding kiss that drowned out every last thought in my mind; the kind of kiss that sent a man over the edge as he chased the pleasure he knew only one woman could give him.

She consumed me.

Body and fucking soul.

Like no one ever had before.

Her legs tightened around me; her fingers dug into my skin; her mouth claimed me, and I would have given her anything she asked for in that moment. Hell, who was I kidding? I'd give her anything she *ever* asked for.

As our lips and tongues worked each other into a frenzy, I thrust inside her, and groaned at how fucking good she felt.

I wanted to live there forever.

I never wanted to let her go again.

Fuck.

I pulled out and thrust in again.

I repeated this over and over, and she took everything I had to give, and gave it all back to me. Our pace intensified and we fucked like we hadn't for months.

Skin on skin.

Lips on lips.

Arms, legs, fingers, clinging, clawing, demanding...

13

"Fuck!" I tore my mouth from hers. "I can't hold it much longer...you almost there?"

She gripped me harder. "Yes..." Her voice was barely a pant as she kept moving with me, desperately chasing her release. And then – "Oh, God, Scott...ohhh...I'm gonna come..."

As the words fell from her lips, her pussy squeezed around my dick, and her eyes fluttered shut, and I watched as she lost herself to her orgasm.

So fucking beautiful.

I thrust twice more and then I let myself go. The intense pleasure surged through me and I was lost to the world in those moments.

Like a fucking drug straight to my veins.

I'm addicted to her.

When I finally gained control, I found her watching me through glazed eyes. I bent my face to hers and kissed her almost as hard as I'd fucked her. "You got any idea what you do to me?" I demanded as I let her lips go. My body buzzed with need and love for this woman. I'd never experienced any of this with any other woman in my life, and there'd never be another like Harlow.

Her lips spread out in a slow smile but she didn't say anything.

She knew; she had to fucking know, because for the last year, I'd laid my heart and soul down for her in ways I'd never laid it down for anyone.

My arm tightened around her and I pulled her harder against me. "You're mine, Harlow. Your heart, your body, *you*...all mine. And that drives me crazy some days."

Her smile shifted into a frown. "Why does that drive you crazy?"

My heart beat faster as I contemplated that question; as I exposed another piece of my heart to her. "You're like a drug, baby. The highs are fuckin' spectacular and I'd go through any low to have those highs. And I'd do anything to make sure I always had you, even if it meant selling my fuckin' soul."

She threaded her fingers through my hair at the back of my head and pressed another kiss to my lips; less demanding this time, more gentle. "I'd take all the lows, too, if it meant I got just one of the highs with you. I love you, Scott."

Fuck, I might have thought she was mine, but I was far more hers than she was mine; she fucking owned me.

I pulled out of her and took a step back so she could move off the counter. When she stood in front of me, I yanked her closer. "Now I want you in the shower. It's time for me to show you what I like to do with dirty mouths." I jerked my chin towards the bathroom. "Go. I'll meet you there in a minute."

Lust shone from her eyes and she nodded before leaving me.

I raked my fingers through my hair as I watched her go, and wondered, not for the first time, when I'd have all

15

the pieces of her back – the pieces that had shattered when she'd lost our baby. The pieces she hadn't been able to find to put back together yet.

I miss those pieces.

As I followed in the direction she'd gone, I vowed yet again to help her find those fucking pieces.

Five hours later, I was sitting outside on the verandah with a beer contemplating club business when Harlow came up behind me, wrapped her arms around me and whispered against my ear, "You wore me out." I'd had her in the shower and then again in our bed, and fuck, I'd worn myself out, too. She'd fallen asleep for a little while, but I'd been unable to switch my brain off.

She came and curled up in my lap. I put one arm around her and rested my hand holding my beer on her bare leg. She wore only a t-shirt of mine and I fought the urge to rip it off her. First we needed to talk. As she rested her head on my shoulder, I asked, "Did you spend time with the girls today?"

I could hear the smile in her voice when she replied. "Yeah, it was quiet at the café and Mum suggested I take some time off after my appointment with Jane. Roxie had some free time so I decided to get my hair done."

Jane, her psychologist, had won my respect even though I'd never believed in that shit before. Harlow had

16

come to life again after starting to see her nearly two months ago. "You had a good appointment with Jane?" I took a swig of my beer while waiting to hear about her appointment. Something in her day today had gone well and I wanted to know what it was.

She lifted her head to look at me. Even the change in her eyes was clear to see. Most days it felt like she looked straight through me, but tonight she was soaking me in. Today I didn't need her words to know I was the man she loved; today her eyes told me everything I needed to know.

Happiness blazed from her. "I had the best appointment with Jane today, but I couldn't even tell you why. It was as if something one of us said just triggered a change in me. You know how sometimes someone can say or do something and it makes you see things differently...well, that's what happened."

"What did she say?"

"She brought up coping mechanisms with me again and you know, I don't think I was really listening all the other times she talked about them. Today it seemed to click into place and I feel like I can do this." The way she gushed her words gave me hope this really might be a turning point. I hadn't heard Harlow talk like this for a long time.

"Do you mean the things like doing yoga, and eating well, and writing shit down?"

Her eyebrows shot up. "Have you been researching it?"

17

I placed my beer on the ground and ran my hand up her leg and over her ass where I let it rest. "I read all the sheets of paper you bring home from her, sweetheart." Hell, I devoured those sheets looking for an answer.

She held my gaze for a few moments before saying anything, and then pressed a kiss to my lips. Just a quick one, but I could feel the love it held. "Thank you," she whispered as if she was thanking me for the world.

I frowned. "For reading that stuff?"

Shaking her head, she corrected me. "No, for loving me enough to get me help, and for coming to the appointments I needed you at, and for reading all those sheets of paper...for giving me the time and space to work myself out. People might think you're a hard ass, but they don't know the real you." She paused and curled her hand around my neck before adding, "I'm the luckiest woman in the world to know the real you." Her lips came to mine again and her kiss was long and deep.

I groaned and gripped her ass while she kissed me. When she finally let my lips go, I said, "Harlow, any man would have done that for you. Any man would want you to be happy again. I'm just doing what they would do."

"No, they wouldn't have. You know about the assholes I've dated before – not one of them would have stood next to me like you did."

Just the thought of those men caused my chest to tighten. "You're right," I said. "Every man but those assholes would have done what I did."

18

She smiled and then her smile morphed into seriousness as she cocked her head to the side. "So are you going to tell me about your day?"

I drew a long breath and then slowly let it out. "We lost some men today. They didn't agree with a club decision and I gave them the option to leave the club, which they chose to do. And on top of that we've got a new drug dealer in town causing trouble so I've gotta deal with him."

"How many members left?"

"Seven."

Her eyes widened. "Goodness - " she started, but I cut her off.

"I don't want you to worry about this. Griff and I have it covered. I just want you to focus on doing the stuff Jane tells you to do so you can get better."

Annoyance flared in her eyes. "Don't do that."

"Do what?" I stared at her waiting for her answer, not sure where she was coming from.

"That thing men sometimes do where they think they're helping their woman by telling her not to worry about what they are going through. Of course I'm going to worry about you and the club so there's no point telling me not to worry. The thing that will make me worry less is if you keep me up-to-date with where you're at with it." She moved off my lap and stared down at me. Usually I'd allow my gaze to travel the length of her body, but the passion she spoke with kept my attention firmly on her

19

face. "I'm going to keep focusing on doing the things Jane spoke to me about, but at the same time I'm going to be thinking about you, so you may as well keep me updated. Otherwise, my imagination will take over and I'll probably picture the worst." Her eyes flashed with passion and her tone was forceful.

She's found some of her pieces.

I moved off the chair, slid my arm around her waist and pulled her close, pressing her body to mine. "You want me to keep you updated, I'm gonna need something from you, too," I growled.

Her breathing picked up and she stared up at me through heated eyes. *This* was the Harlow I needed – the woman who could go from annoyed, to passionate, to turned on in one conversation. "What?" she demanded.

My eyes searched hers for a moment, appreciating the emotion radiating from them. Savouring everything I saw because it had been too long since I'd had it from her, and hoping like fuck to see it every day from here on out. "I'm gonna need you to keep talking to me about where you're at." I held her tight while I waited for her response.

She nodded. "I will." Her promise fell easily from her lips and all I could do was hope she kept it, because this woman standing in front of me was the woman I'd decided to spend the rest of my life with, and I needed her whole again.

I was done marking time and waiting for her to come back to me.

I was done with a lot of things in my life.

It was time to take command and make shit happen.

The next morning, I sat at the head of the table at Church and surveyed the room. My brothers watched me through eyes that betrayed their true feelings. They knew as well as I did that seven men down meant shit could happen that we might not be able to deal with. The thing about Storm, though, was that we would fight till our dying breath to protect what was ours.

"I've called Rogue and Colt home, and we're patching Gunnar in," I announced. Rogue and Colt were nomads, and had both assured me last night they'd be here within two days, if not sooner. If we needed him, I'd also call Havoc but I knew King had work for him in Sydney at the moment.

Everyone agreed, and then Griff spoke. "I've got Nash and J keeping track of every move Julio makes while I investigate him. I can tell you he's from Adelaide and has a sister there. Apart from her, I can't find any other family members. He has a network in South Australia and from what I can work out, he controls the drugs in most of that state."

"So he's probably tied up with Bourne," I mused. *The President of the Adelaide Storm chapter.* The asshole I'd hoped to avoid as much as possible.

"Fuck," J muttered, looking as frustrated as I felt. "I'd hoped we were done with that prick."

I eyed him. "You've got two contacts down there, right?"

"Yeah. You want me to find out what they know?"

Nodding, I said, "See what they know and let's hope like fuck we can get what we need out of them. I want as little to do with Bourne as possible."

"Will do," he agreed.

Turning to Wilder, I asked, "Where are we at with Trilogy?" He was recovering from being shot so I was keeping him on light duties at the moment. Managing the reopening of the restaurant fit this bill.

"It's on track to reopen next week. The staff are pretty much all lined up and ready to go, but we may need to borrow some from the other restaurants until we hire a few more waitresses." The thing I appreciated about Wilder was how he moved on from shit once it was dealt with. After he'd brought the new information on Julio to the table yesterday and I'd had words with him afterwards, it was done as far as he was concerned. It was the way I preferred to operate as well.

"Good work, brother. I want you to take on the job of overseeing the restaurants and Indigo for now. You good with that?"

He gave me a nod. "Consider it done." I had no doubt in his ability; he'd proven himself with getting Trilogy up and running again.

I turned my attention back to the table. "We're done here for today. You've all got your jobs and I want to be kept updated with anything you find out, no matter how insignificant you might think it is. Understood?"

They all agreed and left to get started.

Griff held back and when we were alone, he said, "I'm gonna do some digging on Bourne. I don't think it's a coincidence Julio and he came up in the same conversation today. Marcus was tight with Bourne and they had plans for Brisbane, so it makes me question whether there's any connection."

I rubbed the back of my neck; this had unsettled me, too. "That thought had also crossed my mind."

"I'll let you know what I find out."

He'd walked the few steps to the door when I asked, "You free this weekend? I need some help fixing a fence."

"Yours?"

"The fence on Michelle's house." It was the house next door to mine; the house I owned and rented out to Michelle.

"How's she going these days? Still clean?"

"As far as I know she is. I haven't seen any signs to say otherwise and Harlow keeps an eye out, too. Fuck knows, Michelle needs it – she has no family to look out for her, and her friends are mostly junkies that she's tried to distance herself from. I'll give her credit – she has made a huge effort to clean herself up."

23

"Good to hear. I might not be in town this weekend. I'll have to let you know on Friday whether I can help."

I narrowed my eyes at him. "Where are you going?" Griff didn't leave town often, if ever.

"Could be heading down to Byron for the weekend."

I frowned. "When the fuck do you go to Byron?"

A scowl flitted across his face. "This weekend; that's when the fuck," he snapped, and I knew from his tone and the hard set of his shoulders that this conversation was over.

A moment later he exited the room and I wondered what the hell was going on with him. However, all thoughts of that left my mind when I entered the bar a couple of minutes later to find J and Wilder watching the surveillance from the camera we had on the outside of the building.

J eyed me with a grin. "Get a look at this, brother."

I stepped closer to the screen to see what they were watching. A dark haired woman stood in the car park and looked to be arguing with Nash over something. And she looked to be winning that argument.

"Looks like she's giving Nash a piece of her mind," J said with a snicker.

We watched them for another couple of minutes until I realised how agitated Nash was getting. When he took a step away from her and she followed, I knew the time had come to get involved.

J came with me, and when we reached them, Nash was saying – "Babe, we had nothing to do with the drugs your brother bought, so for fuck's sake take your argument to whoever did."

Now that I was able to get a good look at the woman, I saw she was only young – early twenties at the most. She wore shorts and a t-shirt, and tattoos covered her thighs and arms. Her long dark hair hung like wild chaos around her in a similar fashion to the anger she'd brought with her.

Her brows rose behind the dark glasses covering her eyes. "He told me he bought them from Storm and that he owed you money. I've come here today to pay you the goddamn money and to ask you...no, to fucking *beg* you, to stop selling him the drugs so he can try to get clean again." While anger clothed her, desperation blazed between her words – her anxiety to clear the debt rang out loud and clear.

Nash opened his mouth to reply, but I spoke before he could. "Consider whatever debt he thought he had, cleared."

Her mouth fell open for a moment before she snapped it closed and ripped her sunglasses from her face. Untrusting brown eyes glared back at me. "Bullshit. Bikers don't just clear debts."

"This one does." Figuring she was far from the kind of woman to back down easily, I waited for her to continue the argument.

Shaking her head at me, she ran her fingers through her wavy hair. "Fuck," she muttered. "Look, I've got shit to do so, for the love of God, will you just let me pay you?" Narrowing her eyes at me, she added, "Honestly, what kind of drug dealer turns money down?"

She was beginning to piss me off. I moved closer to her so I was in her space. Bending my face closer to hers, I said, "I'm - "

Before I could get my words out, she kneed me in the balls and after placing her hands against my chest, shoved me hard so I stumbled backwards.

Fuck.

I hadn't seen that coming and fuck if I'd let it go without giving her a piece of my mind.

Wild eyes stared at me, and her chest rose and fell hard and fast as she spat out, "Don't fucking come that close to me again."

Heat flushed through me as my body tensed with anger and pain. "You need to get the fuck off my property now and never come back. We don't sell drugs here. Get your facts right before you come around accusing people of shit they didn't do and if you ever fuckin' touch my balls again, be prepared for the repercussions." I fumed as I glared at her, waiting for her to leave.

She met my glare and didn't let go. Instead of doing what I'd said, she grabbed an envelope out of her bag and slapped it into my hand. "I'm not accusing you of anything; I couldn't give a shit what people do to make a living. All I want is the debt cleared and my brother left alone. You think you can manage that?"

J whistled. "Fuck, the girl's got balls."

I didn't take my eyes off her. Either J was right or she was dumb as fuck; I was tending towards J being right. As we watched each other, a car pulled into the car park, pulling my attention away for a second.

Harlow.

She parked her car and made her way to where the four of us stood. Frowning, she asked, "What's going on?"

"I was just leaving," the girl muttered, taking a step back as she watched Harlow with the same level of distrust she'd looked at us with.

"You don't need to leave on my account," Harlow said. "I just dropped in for a quick hello; nothing important, so I can wait inside for you to be done."

As she made a move to leave us, I snagged her around the waist and pulled her to me. "I won't be long, sweetheart," I said, my eyes holding hers. Fuck, whatever perfume she had on today smelt amazing.

A lazy smile spread across her face. Standing on her toes, she brushed a quick kiss across my lips. "See you soon," she murmured before pulling out of my hold and walking inside.

My gaze followed her until I could no longer see her. Turning back to the girl, I snapped, "You should go."

Her eyes glinted with displeasure. "My thoughts exactly," she muttered before sweeping one last glare over all of us and turning to walk towards her car parked on the road.

The three of us watched her go before Nash looked at me and said, "Jesus fucking Christ, I hope to God we never see her again."

"Yeah, you and Scott's balls hope to never see her again," J chipped in as he smirked.

I raked my fingers through my hair as the tension punched through my body. I'd been on edge when she arrived and she'd only amplified that. Holding up the envelope she'd given me, I said, "What's the bet it was Keg who sold to her brother?"

"I figured that, too," J said.

"I'll hold onto this in case she comes back looking for it." Although I figured it had been Keg who sold the drugs, if someone else did, they'd go looking for this cash and she'd need it then.

We headed back inside and I found Harlow waiting for me at the bar. She held Wilder's and Griff's attention, and I took a moment to appreciate the ease with which she got on with club members. She'd kept away from the clubhouse over the past few months, choosing to lock herself away at home or at the café. Seeing her here today, laughing like she was, made me happy.

She smiled at me as I approached, and turned her body to mine when I stood in front of her. "I missed you this morning." Her voice was soft; all breathy like she'd been thinking of fucking me.

28

I bent my head so my mouth was near her ear. "Damn, woman, you know that sexy voice of yours gets me hard." I spoke so that only she could hear, but I didn't give a fuck if anyone else heard it. My feelings for Harlow weren't something I ever tried to hide.

Her body swayed and her back arched as the front of her brushed up against me. "I could take care of that right now." Her eyes flirted with mine and her promise sizzled in the air between us.

Fuck.

Yes.

I grabbed hold of her hand and without another glance at anyone in the room, I stalked towards the office, pulling her with me. No fucking way could a man pass up that offer.

When we arrived at the office, I ushered her inside and kicked the door closed behind us. Then I pushed her against the desk and reached for the button on her jeans. "Fuck, sweetheart, why'd you wear jeans? A skirt would be better for this kind of thing." I moved as fast as I could to undo her jeans because, hell, my dick had hardened to the point where a man could go crazy if he didn't get any relief.

She raised her brows. "Really? You're gonna complain about shit when I'm standing in front of you offering you *this*?" As she said the word 'this', she guided my hand to her pussy.

Her wet, dripping pussy.

29

Fuck.

I ran my finger through her lips and groaned. "Not complaining, Harlow, just stating the fuckin' truth." I yanked her jeans down and then her panties. "Did you wake up wet for me, baby?"

She'd undone my jeans and pulled my cock out. Wrapping her hand around it, she began stroking me. "Yes, and you were gone so I took care of myself with BOB, but he's never enough. Especially not when I make myself come thinking about you; it just makes me need you more."

I groaned again; the thought of her using a vibrator turned me on, but her dirty talking took me to a whole new level of turned on. Grinding myself against her, I growled, "From now on, I'll wake you up and fuck you before I leave for work." As the words left my mouth, I lifted her so she sat on the desk, thrust my cock inside her and squeezed my eyes shut as her pussy welcomed me in.

God damn, my woman felt good.

She moaned and dug her fingers into my back. "Fuck me hard, Scott. Fast and hard," she pleaded. Desire laced her words and caused me to move with clear intention. If Harlow wanted fast and hard, who the fuck was I to argue?

Her legs wrapped around me and we lost ourselves while we gave our bodies over to the pleasure we craved. There was no kissing and no gentleness to this sex; it was raw need, pure and simple.

30

Cock and pussy and cum.

A quick fuck that would get us through the day until I could fuck her until she passed out tonight.

As her orgasm shattered through her, she clung to me tighter, digging her fingers into my skin even harder. No words escaped her mouth, but her breathing had quickened and I watched as her eyes closed and she bit her bottom lip. And then my orgasm moved through my body, and I thrust one last time before coming.

Fuck.

I tightened my hold on her and dropped my head against her shoulder. We didn't move for a few minutes, but eventually I pulled out and let her go. I pulled my jeans up and loved the fuck out of it when her hands took over and did them up. Her eyes didn't leave mine, and hell if they didn't promise me all sorts of sexy shit.

"Christ, it's like you're making up for lost time," I said as she pulled her panties and jeans up.

"Are you complaining?" The playfulness in her tone told me she loved this conversation.

I dropped my lips to hers and kissed her. It was a long, deep kiss and when we finally surfaced for air, I said, "Fuck, no. Anytime you want to make up for lost time, just call me, and I'm there."

She grinned and reached for her bag that she'd dumped on my desk. Pulling something out that was wrapped in tin foil, she placed it in my hands. "You need to eat this because I'm going to bake your other favourite tonight."

I frowned. "What's my other favourite?"

Shaking her head, she refused to tell me. "You'll have to wait until tonight if you don't know what it is. It'll be a surprise that I guarantee you'll love." She pressed another kiss to my lips before slinging her bag over her shoulder and taking a step away from me.

I placed the cake on the desk and folded my arms across my chest. Watching as she took the few steps to the door, I said, "A head's up, sweetheart – my dick is already hard for you again. That sweet pussy of yours is mine tonight and I plan on fucking you all night long, so take it easy today."

Her steps faltered and when she turned to me, I could clearly see how much my words had affected her.

Almost as much as just thinking about her affected me.

"I love your filthy mouth, Scott Cole," she said, and with that she left.

I pushed off the desk and looked out the window, watching as she left the clubhouse a few minutes later. So many thoughts filled my mind, but as they came and went, one thought remained.

It's good to have my woman back.

Chapter Two
Harlow

Today is going to be a good day.

I repeated this over and over in my mind as I drove away from the clubhouse. Yesterday I'd felt like I could conquer the world, but today I felt like the world could conquer me. It made no sense to me because after a great day yesterday and an amazing night with Scott, I'd thought for sure I would wake up today and tackle everything head on. But then again, the thing I'd learnt over the past few months was that not much in my head made sense to me.

I'd woken up with that empty feeling in the pit of my stomach that I'd become used to. Empty and me were old friends. The difference now, though, was that it was a friendship I had become determined to end. So I'd plastered a smile on my face and gone to see my man because the other thing I'd learnt over the past few months was that Scott was there for me in any way I needed. I'd never known a man to be that loyal, but he'd shown me I could have full faith in him. He'd also made it clear he wanted me to lean on him and be open with him. I'd fully intended to do that this morning – to tell him my high from yesterday had disappeared – but when he'd been turned on just from being near me, it had made me feel so good that I went along with it and shoved the rest from my mind.

Today is going to be a good day.

Half an hour later, I sat at a table in the corner of a little café I'd discovered recently. Mum had given me the day off and I was at a loss as to what to do with myself. Life had been crazy busy lately between working at the café, which was hectic at the moment, and doing night shifts at Indigo. Between the two jobs and doing my best to get through each day, I hadn't had much time to myself. Today was a gift from my Mum and I didn't want to waste it, but the options of how to spend my time jostled for my attention and I felt overwhelmed trying to choose.

34

In the end, I'd decided to find a quiet corner at the café, drink some coffee and do some journaling. Getting my thoughts out of my mind and onto paper always helped give me some clarity.

I was deeply engrossed in my thoughts when my best friend, Cassie, phoned. "I just spoke to your mum and she told me you have the day off. What are you doing?"

"I'm sitting in a café, journaling. Apart from that, I have no idea what I'm going to do." I sighed. This should not be so hard.

She remained quiet for a moment. "You could go make some art." She'd been quietly suggesting this to me for weeks and I had been avoiding discussing it with her. Picking up a paintbrush had been the last thing I wanted to do.

"Cassie," I started and then stopped when she made a strange noise on the other end of the phone – it was the noise she made when she was about to argue with me. I leant my elbow on the table and rested my head against my hand. "Go on, say what you need to say." I settled in to listen to her thoughts; she'd been far too quiet on this for far too long and I was sure she had something to say.

"Girl, you know I love you and I would do anything for you, and that's why I *have* to say this to you now. I truly believe your art will help you cope with everything you're struggling with at the moment. We were working towards selling some of your paintings and then you got pregnant, which caused you to put everything aside while you were making plans for the baby. And I get that, but art to you, Harlow, is like air to me. It's how you used to get through your days, and I think you've forgotten that."

I sat up straight and let her words circle through me. "I'm not ready to start selling my art, Cassie." *She'd* been the one working towards selling my art - the thought actually struck fear through me. *What if people hate it?*

"I'm not saying you need to sell it; I'm just saying you need to make it. For you. For your soul."

My psychologist had said the same thing, but she didn't know me as well as Cassie did, so she hadn't pushed me on it. My best friend, on the other hand, would push me. Best thing I could do right now was tell her I'd consider it. "I'll think about it, Cass."

"Promise me you will. In fact, promise me you'll go home and sit in your art room while you think about it."

"Okay, okay! I will go and sit in my room. God, you're a pushy bitch."

She laughed. "I swear if you don't do this, my last resort will be telling Scott what I think. And we both know he's bossy enough to take your ass into that room and put a paintbrush in your hand. I'm actually surprised he hasn't done that already."

"He's had a lot going on with the club. And he still does, so please don't bug him with this; he doesn't need anymore headaches."

"From what I know about your man, I'm pretty sure he'd want to be bugged about anything concerning you.

I'm going to check in with you tonight to see where you're at."

We ended the call and I let out a long breath. I loved my best friend, but sometimes she pushed me when I didn't want to be pushed. Just because someone thought they knew what was best for you didn't make them right. Sometimes we had thoughts and feelings locked away from everyone that if they knew, they'd understand why we couldn't yet do what they wanted us to do.

Art might have been like air to me, but my greatest fear was that breathing again might cripple me. Art had a way of unlocking the parts of my soul I kept even from myself. It took a strong woman to confront those kinds of buried truths, and I wasn't sure I was strong enough at the moment.

I remember the first day I realised art was my therapy. Sixteen at the time and working through my grief over losing my father, I'd locked myself away every afternoon after school and painted. I'd shut my friends out, but I hadn't missed them, and I'd actually discovered I needed time with myself to heal. Some people needed to surround themselves with others to get through the hard parts of their lives, but I was the opposite – I needed to go within.

Mixing colours, playing with different techniques and allowing my soul to wash itself over the canvas had been my saviour.

After my conversation with Cassie, I'd left the café and headed home. I wasn't sure I'd drag my paint out, but I'd sit in my art room and think. Maybe I'd journal. I'd at least go in there, even if only to be able to tell her I'd done what she'd asked. I didn't want her harassing Scott with this. Not when he needed to be focused completely on Storm.

My art room sat perfectly organised and tidy, nothing out of place. Scott had cleared out his spare room when I'd moved in so I could set myself up in here, but I'd hardly used it. I eyed the bookshelf that held my paints. So much beautiful colour in one place. Moving to the bookshelf, I picked up a tube of turquoise and unscrewed the lid. I squeezed the tube and allowed some paint to escape onto my finger. I then reached for one of my art journals and swiped the paint onto a random page.

My body stilled as I stared at the page in front of me. I'd expected a rush of inspiration or a feeling or a thought or something. *Anything.* Instead, empty taunted me.

Make it stop!

I don't want to feel this way anymore.

Stepping away from the bookshelf with the paint, I moved to the desk and dropped the art journal on it. I yanked the chair out and slumped onto it. In frustration, I reached for a pen and began scrawling random words and sentences onto the page with the swipe of turquoise across it.

Why do I feel so lost?

Blank.

Suffering.

When will this end?

What is wrong with me?

Hope.

I will get better.

I feel like I've lost myself.

A tear splashed onto the page and another one sat on my eyelash. I didn't wipe them away. They needed to fall. *I need to fall.*

I put the pen down and flipped to the first page in the journal. Settling back into the chair, I began to go through my art and read what I'd written. This was the last journal I'd worked on before I had my miscarriage so it held my most recent thoughts.

Over the next hour, I devoured not only this journal, but a few of my other ones. When I was finished, I pulled my legs up so my feet rested on the chair, and wrapped my arms around my legs. And I let the tears fall.

The woman who had bared her soul in those journals was not the woman I was today.

How did I change so much in such a short period of time?

That woman had confidence and faith and belief.

I have none.

I'd been going through the motions of life since my miscarriage and had been so consumed by the daily grind of life that I'd forgotten to live.

Where do I even start to find myself again?

I shoved the chair back and stood. God, I was seriously annoying myself with the back and forth of emotions. This couldn't be healthy for anyone. *Could it?* Raking my fingers through my hair, I blew out a long, pissed off breath.

I wanted to scream.

I wanted to kick something.

I wanted the madness in my mind to stop!

Stalking back to the bookshelf housing the paints, I grabbed as many tubes as I could hold and carried them back to the desk. I then opened my art journal again, picked up a paintbrush, and painted.

I had no idea what I'd paint – I simply let the art take over and allowed my soul to spill onto the page.

Hours passed.

I didn't stop to eat.

I kept on painting.

Vibrant colour filled my pages and at some point, I moved to canvas.

More hours passed.

I moved to the floor of my art room.

When I finally looked up after a noise splintered my attention, the sky outside was dark, and paint covered not only my journal and three canvases, but also my skin.

Scott stood in the doorway to my art room with his arms folded across his chest and his feet planted wide. "Have you been in here all day?"

I blinked, disoriented. Frowning, I asked, "What time is it?"

"It's just after seven." His gaze shifted to take in the room; to take in the mess I'd created. My art supplies were strewn across the floor and over my desk.

I hardly remember making this mess.

Standing, I stepped over my supplies and walked to where he stood. Placing my hand on his chest, I apologised, "Sorry, I haven't even thought about dinner yet."

His hand caught mine as I shifted it off his chest. Not moving his gaze from mine, he said, "Sweetheart, I could give a fuck about dinner."

Guilt filtered through me. Even though he didn't care, I did. I wanted to be the woman he needed, and I wanted to look after him as well as he looked after me.

Before I could say anything, he placed a finger under my chin and tilted my face to his. "What are you thinking?" His voice was firm but gentle as he guided me to give him what he wanted.

I blinked again. "I know you don't care about dinner, but I do. I should have cooked us something."

A look crossed his face. If I had to take a guess, I would have said it was frustration. His jaw ticked and I waited for him to let his frustration loose, but he didn't. Instead, he said, "I'll cook dinner while you get cleaned up."

His tone held no room for argument so I nodded. "Okay."

He let me go and stepped aside to let me through. As I exited the room, he added, "And Harlow?" I turned back to see what he had to say. "When you're finished cleaning up, I want you in the kitchen with me while I cook. I don't know what the fuck is going on in your head tonight, but what I do know is that it needs to stop. I've gone easy on you over the past few months and I'm done with easy." And there was the Scott Cole I knew well.

My bossy man.

Fifteen minutes later, I joined Scott in the kitchen. I'd had so much paint on my skin and in my hair that I'd decided to shower. He looked up from the vegetables he was slicing to give me his attention.

I slid onto the stool across from him and leant my elbows on the kitchen counter. "What are you cooking?"

"Steak and veggies." His gaze roamed over me and butterflies fluttered in my belly. When he finally gave me back his eyes, he said, "Start talking, baby."

I sighed. "Can we talk about this later? I want to know about your day."

42

He shook his head and squared his shoulders in the way he did when he was settling in for the kind of discussion where he intended to be forceful. "No."

We watched each other intently and my heart beat a little faster. Admitting you felt lost and like a failure to the man you loved was not an easy thing to do. I never wanted Scott to look at me in any way other than the way he always had, and I worried that if he knew I wasn't all he thought I was, he'd look at me differently.

"Harlow, start talking." His words came out almost as a growl and I knew my time had run out. I had to give him something.

Shit.

My head buzzed with dizzying lightness, but I pushed on and started talking. "I'm not where I thought I would be by now..." I faltered on my words and swallowed back my nervousness. At his frown, I continued. "I mean, my life hasn't gone the way I thought it would."

He raised his brows and placed the knife he was holding down. Resting his hands on the kitchen counter, he said, "Go on."

God, I was making a mess of this. "That came out wrong, Scott. I don't mean *you* – you're the best thing in my life. I never want to lose you and I never want our relationship to change. It's important to me that I don't mess us up." My words were coming out fast and I stopped to take a breath.

His chest rose as he also took a breath – a long, deep breath that signalled the frustration he was holding back. "Where did you think you'd be by now?"

I moved off the stool and walked around the island bench to where he stood. His eyes tracked my every movement and I knew from the intense way he watched me that I needed to find the right words to express what I was feeling.

I placed my hand on his chest and then ran it down his t-shirt before grasping his shirt in my hand; needing to maintain closeness to him. "I was raised a good country girl, Scott, and in the country we get married young, and have kids. Family is everything and it's something I've always wanted. But I made so many bad choices where men were concerned -" I ignored the way his nostrils flared and the way his vein pulsed in his neck, " – that I had begun to wonder if I'd ever find a good man. Instead, I started to concentrate on my art and thought about trying to make a living from it. But then I found you and fell pregnant, and changed course again. I was so excited to be pregnant even though it wasn't something you and I had planned. And then I lost our baby, and well, we all know where that ended up." I took a breath. "I feel like I've failed all the way around," I admitted softly.

His brows pulled together as he processed everything I'd said. "You haven't failed. I mean, fuck, losing a baby by no fault of your own is not what I'd call failing - "

I tugged on his shirt and cut him off. "I'm not saying the way I am feeling is *right*. I'm just trying to explain to you where I'm at. I know I have a lot of work to do on my thinking, and myself, but you asked what I was thinking today, and that's it." Spending the day going through my journals and then painting had unlocked a range of emotions and shed some light on where the churning in my gut was coming from. Unlike I'd assumed, my unhappiness didn't just stem from losing a baby.

"Damn straight it's not right," he said with force and I loved my man even more in that moment. His faith in me was astounding some days. Having a man in your corner like I did was everything, especially on the days where you felt like you'd been beaten into that corner by the blows life dealt.

I smiled. "I also need to tell you that I came to see you this morning because I was feeling down. I thought I'd turned a corner yesterday and then last night with you was amazing so I went to bed thinking today was going to be another great day. But I woke up feeling low, which sucked."

"Fuck, it's like a damn rollercoaster, isn't it?"

"Yeah, but I'm not going to let it get the best of me." And I wouldn't; now that I'd remembered the parts of me I'd forgotten, I'd fight to find them again. Regardless of how hard the journey would be.

He took hold of my hand that held his shirt. "Your art helped today?"

45

I nodded. "Yes, it always does."

Cocking his head to the side, he asked, "Why didn't you do it sooner?"

"I don't think I was ready for it," I admitted. "It wasn't a conscious decision, but I think I knew deep down that my art would bring all the hard stuff I have to deal with to the surface. And I think I had to move through my feelings about our baby first."

"This bullshit about you feeling like you should have cooked dinner? That's gotta stop, babe. I'd rather you spend time figuring your head out through your art than cooking me dinner." Scott always seemed to have the ability to say the exact right thing to me when I needed to hear it. Even if it sometimes came out in his trademark bossy way.

I moved into him so our bodies touched – my favourite place to be. Reaching up, I curled my hand around his neck and pulled his face down to mine so I could kiss him. His mouth opened with hesitation and we found each other in the one place we never failed to find each other. Being in his arms reminded me of what I held important.

When he ended the kiss, he held my face and ran his thumb over my cheek. "I know I'm a hard-ass, and I probably don't say shit very well, but I need you to know that the only thing I want is for you to get back to being you. I don't want you to worry about me or looking after me by cooking and shit; that's not important at the moment. Let me do all the worrying for the moment; let me help get you through this."

I nodded. "I will. I'm not the kind of person who is good with letting someone else carry my load, but I'm trying to share it."

His eyes narrowed on me. "When you talked about having a family before, does that mean you want to try again for a baby?"

"I've thought a lot about it, but I'm still not sure how I feel about trying again just yet." My mind was still a mess of confusion on this so I figured the best thing to do was keep working through my feelings before rushing into it.

"Okay. We don't need to speed shit up; when you're ready we'll talk more about it."

"How do you feel about it?" In all of my depression and pulling away from him, we'd hardly discussed how he felt and I was mad at myself for not considering his feelings more.

"Harlow, if you asked me for fuckin' triplets tomorrow, I'd do everything in my power to make that shit happen. I want a family with you, baby, and whether that happens this year or in five years, I don't mind, so long as I have you. And so long as you're happy." The way he looked at me with his serious eyes that didn't blink, and the way his body had pressed against me again revealed the truth in his words.

Happiness flared from deep within and my tummy fluttered. "I know I'm on this rollercoaster of emotions at

47

the moment, but I need you to know that *you* make me happy. And more than anything, I'm looking forward to the day we begin adding to our family."

If I'd thought his words had made me happy before, what he did next only added to that. He smiled. It was only a small Scott-Cole-kind-of-smile, but at the same time, his eyes crinkled. I hadn't seen his crinkles for a while now, and I'd missed them. He then dropped his lips to mine and claimed me again.

As our kiss deepened, his hands moved down my body, skimming my curves and circling my waist before resting on my ass. He groaned a moment later when his phone rang. I wanted to tell him to ignore it, but I knew it could be something important to do with the club so I let him go and tried to step out of his hold. However, he frowned down at me as I tried, and his hand tightened its hold on me, keeping my body close to his.

He checked his caller ID before answering, and then said, "Lisa, what's up, darlin'?"

As Lisa spoke, his eyes met mine, concerned, and he finally let me go. "I'm coming over now," he said and hung up.

"What's up?" I watched as he shoved his phone in his jeans pocket.

"Michelle's sick and Lisa is worried about her. Says Michelle hasn't woken up since she got home from school and that she's burning up."

"Do you want me to come with you?"

48

"No, can you finish cooking dinner while I do this? We've got enough there for Lisa to eat; I'm guessing she hasn't had dinner yet."

"Good idea."

I watched him leave and then turned my attention to dinner. Ten minutes later, I had all the vegetables chopped and the meat ready to cook when I heard a crashing sound on the back deck. Stilling, I listened closely to see if I could work out what had caused it.

Crash!

I had no idea what it was, and my natural instinct to investigate kicked in. Reaching into one of the kitchen drawers, I pulled out the rolling pin; if there was someone out there, I wouldn't hesitate to use it.

Treading silently, I made my way to the back door and opened it. No more noises had sounded so I remained hopeful no one would surprise me, but when I flicked on the light, a tall, well-built man loomed in front of me.

"Oh my God!" I screamed and let the rolling pin loose on him.

His arm shot up to stop my weapon from hitting him, and he easily yanked it out of my hand. "Fuck, woman, go easy." His deep voice sounded pissed off, which annoyed the hell out of me.

"Buddy, this is *my* house, not yours," I snapped as I folded my arms across my chest. "Who the hell are you? And why are you standing on my back deck?" I glared at

49

him while I waited for an answer, taking in the Storm cut he wore.

"Last I knew, this was Scott Cole's place." He frowned. "And last I knew, Scott Cole didn't date, so if this is your place and you're not fucking Scott, where the hell is he?"

"Rogue." Scott's voice sounded behind me, and his arm slid around my waist from behind.

The guy eyed Scott and jerked his chin at me as he said, "Got yourself a firecracker there, mate."

"Why are you holding a rolling pin?" Scott asked.

"Your woman here tried to knock me out with it."

"Well, if you hadn't been crashing around out here in the dark, I wouldn't have had to do that," I muttered, feeling irritated with this Rogue dude and not even sure why.

"Babe, Lisa's inside waiting for dinner. You wanna go take care of that?" Scott's warm breath tickling my neck as he spoke would usually cause my tummy to flutter, but the irritation coursing through me prevented that this time.

I turned in his hold and nodded. "Yeah, I'll leave you two guys to catch up. Is Michelle okay?"

"She's running a fever so I dosed her up on medication. I'll go back later and check on her." He gave me a quick kiss. "Thanks for sorting out dinner for Lisa while I do this."

I gave him a smile. "No worries."

I'd barely left them when I heard Scott giving Rogue hell for swearing at me earlier. I didn't need him to fight my battles for me, but I loved him for it anyway.

Chapter Three
Scott

"You want me to take you to work today?" I leant my shoulder against the doorjamb of the bathroom and watched as Harlow applied her makeup. My gaze trailed down her body, admiring the dress she wore today. The way it barely covered her thighs caused my dick to harden, and I mentally calculated whether I had time to fuck her again before she had to go to work.

"You're thinking about sex again, aren't you?"

My eyes met hers in the mirror. "Sweetheart, when I'm standing this far from you, there's not much on my mind *but* sex. I'm fuckin' counting the ways I can make you come."

Her body stilled and she sucked in a breath. "Maybe you should list them."

I took the few steps to her and pressed myself up against her back, grinding my dick against her ass, and reached a hand under her dress. Pushing her feet apart with one of mine, I skimmed a finger along the edge of her panties. I growled against her ear, "Maybe we should skip the conversation and get straight to the part where I make you scream my name." As I said this, I slid my hand into her panties and dipped my finger into her wet pussy. "It's not gonna take long to make you scream, is it?" I pressed my finger against her sensitive spot and ran it in a circular motion while keeping my gaze glued to the mirror. Watching Harlow lose herself was the best foreplay.

Her head dropped back onto my shoulder and I moved my spare hand to wrap it around her neck. The moan that escaped her lips when I did this reminded me how much she loved a little rough play so I tightened my grip on her.

She surprised the fuck out of me when she reached a hand into her panties and began massaging her clit while I continued to fuck her with my finger. Her hand moving under mine while we both worked her towards an orgasm was hot as hell. Sex with Harlow had always been off the charts good for me, and one of the things I'd always loved was her almost innocence. She was no prude and no beginner, but from what I'd figured, she'd never been fucked dirty before. I fucking loved being the first man to open her up to new experiences. Her hand under mine now was something she'd never done before, and it turned me the fuck on.

As her finger circled her clit, she rocked back and forth, hitting my dick with her sweet ass each time. Her eyes had squeezed closed and she bit her lip.

Fuck, she's perfect.

I let go of her neck and ran my hand down her body so I could cup her breast through her dress. As I rubbed her nipple through her dress, I thought about how much I fucking wanted this dress off her body. Bending my mouth to her ear, I said, "I can't hold off much longer, baby. I need to get the fuck inside you."

Her eyes remained closed as she let out a low moan and circled her hips again. *Fuck me...sexy as fuck.* "I need you in me, too, Scott. I want you to fuck me on the vanity."

She let out another moan.

And bit her lip harder.

And circled her hips around again.

Jesus. Fucking. Christ.

I moved faster than I'd ever moved, and a moment later, I had her on the vanity in front of me with her dress hiked up and her panties off. My pants were down around my ankles and my dick was inside her.

And I fucked her harder than I'd fucked her in months.

Our bodies slammed together as we pushed each other towards our release.

And I just about lost all sanity as a rush of emotions and pleasure burst through me. It was like I'd been holding back for months, not willing to allow myself to fully feel everything going on between us. I'd been so tense with worry, but now she'd come back to me, I could let all that go. I could lose myself in the sex and love and hope.

We're going to be okay. We're going to get through this. Together.

"Scott!" she finally came, screaming my name as her body jerked in my arms. "Oh God...baby...fuck..."

"Fuck!" I rasped as my orgasm hit. Clinging to her, I thrust hard one last time and then gripped the edge of the vanity with both hands as I closed my eyes and let the pleasure take over.

When I was done, I opened my eyes to find her arms wrapped around me and her eyes staring into mine. She hit me with a sexy smile and said, "That was amazing. I want that every morning." Her words hit me square in the chest. They were words I would have given up breath to hear.

I dropped my head and closed my eyes again for a moment as I got my shit together.

"Scott?"

Looking back up, I found her watching me with a slight frown. "I want that every morning, too." I pulled out of her and took a step backwards. Raking my fingers through my hair, I said, "Fuck, do you know how good it is to hear you say that?"

She blinked and I worried for a moment that she was about to cry, but then she gave me another smile. "I bet it's nowhere near as good as having your cock inside me."

"Jesus, Harlow, where's this dirty mouth of yours coming from?"

Her brows raised. "What? You don't like it?" She jumped down off the vanity and retrieved her panties off the floor.

I pulled my pants on and did them up. "I fuckin' love it."

"Good. And, ummm, I think I live with a man who has the dirtiest mouth I've ever heard so that's probably where mine is coming from," she said with a wink.

I finished dressing and then left her to finish getting ready. She found me in the kitchen ten minutes later and as she reached for her car keys, I said, "You don't want me to take you?"

"No, I've gotta do some extra hours with Mum at the café tonight so we can give the kitchen a good clean, and then I've got a shift at Indigo, so I'll just head straight to the club after I finish with Mum. I'll drive myself to save stuffing you around."

I frowned. "I thought you were winding your shifts at Indigo back."

56

She grabbed an apple out of the fruit bowl and bit into it before saying, "I was, but Wilder rang yesterday and asked me if I could pick up some shifts for a little bit while he borrowed staff for Trilogy."

"I'll talk to Wilder and organise something else. I don't want you working so many hours."

Pulling a face at me and placing her hand on her hip, she said, "No, just let me do it, Scott. Wilder's pulling his hair out trying to organise the rosters. He said he's got interviews lined up for later this week so I'm sure he'll find new staff soon, and then I can cut back."

I wanted to argue with her. I wanted to lay down the law, and tell her I wouldn't let her do those hours, but something held me back. Fuck knew what, because it wasn't in my nature to let something like this go, but I did. Instead, I took charge another way. "I'll take you, no ifs or buts." I grabbed my keys and shrugged my cut on before ushering her outside to my bike.

"Wait, didn't you say you were taking Lisa to school this morning?"

Shit.

"Yeah, I did." I checked my watch. "I could take you and then come back to get her."

She shook her head and reached into her bag for her keys. "That will take too much of your time and besides, I think you'd be pushing it. I'll just drive myself, baby." Standing on her toes, she kissed me before heading towards the garage.

I watched her reverse out of the driveway before making my way next door. She'd been right – I wouldn't have had time to take her to work – but no way was I letting her drive herself home after working two shifts today. I'd figure that out later.

Lisa answered the door a few minutes later and gave me one of her sad smiles. "Hi, Scott," she greeted me and let me in.

"Why the sad smile, darlin'?" I wasn't used to seeing them on her these days; now that Michelle was getting her shit together, Lisa was much happier.

"Mum's still not feeling better." She led me into the kitchen where she had her bag half-packed on the kitchen counter.

"Is she awake?"

"Yeah."

"I'll go check on her. Did you give her some more Advil?" At her nod, I left her to go and check on Michelle.

I found her asleep on her bed, but she must have only been dozing because her eyes opened when she heard me enter. "Scott..." Sweat beaded on her forehead and her t-shirt clung to her.

Moving to her wardrobe to find a clean t-shirt, I said, "You look like hell. Are you feeling worse than yesterday?"

"About the same. I'm just so tired, I can hardly keep my eyes open."

I found a t-shirt and turned back to her. Deciding she could do with some cooling off, I left her to go and grab a wet washer. When I returned, she'd curled into a ball. I sat on the edge of her bed and attempted to roll her onto her back. Looking after Michelle wasn't something new to me; Harlow and I had helped her get off the drugs and that had been hell for all of us. I'd seen her at her very worst – strung out, naked, vomiting – so this was like a walk in the park. However, I was aware we needed to get her fever down.

Once I'd rolled her onto her back, I pressed the washer to her forehead, placed the t-shirt on the bed next to her, and said, "Here's a clean shirt. You hungry?"

She shook her head but didn't say anything.

"Scott." Lisa's voice sounded behind me.

Turning my head, I eyed her. "What's up?"

She hesitated for a moment. "I need a note for school to say I can't do sport today. Can you write it?" Her voice betrayed her; something was wrong.

Standing, I walked her way. "Sure, but why aren't you doing sport?" I hoped to hell it didn't have anything to do with the bitches that had bullied her last year. She'd just started high school and as far as I knew, those girls had been leaving her alone.

Her gaze dropped to the ground and the shame that filled her voice when she spoke killed me. "Mum hasn't been able to afford to buy me a sports uniform yet and the teacher for that class is really mean to me about it." She

59

raised her face to look at me. "If I have a note then I can just go to the library rather than have to go to his class and see him."

I pulled my wallet out. "How much is a uniform, darlin'?"

Her eyes widened. "No, I don't want you to buy me a uniform. Mum will have the money next week. I just need a note."

I nodded. "Yeah, so she can pay me back then, but you need a uniform now, so how much?" I dug a fifty out. "Is this enough?"

Embarrassment filled her features, which surprised me. We'd been through a lot together over the years; she shouldn't have felt that way with me. She finally nodded. "Yeah, that's enough."

As she took the money from me, I said, "If you need more, just tell me, okay?" At her nod, I added, "Lisa, I've known you for years, and I know you're going through girl shit and teen shit, but, darlin', there's no judgement between us ever. Whatever you need, I want to know, and I'll make sure you have it. And if it *is* girl stuff you want to talk about, that you don't think I'd get, Harlow's always there for you. Yeah?"

She stared at me for a beat before saying, "Thank you." And then she asked, "Is Harlow okay? I walked in on her crying the other day. I figured it probably had to do with the baby, but I wasn't sure."

Lisa knew about Harlow's miscarriage, but none of us had ever really spoken about it. Mostly because Harlow hadn't really wanted to talk to anyone about her loss, but also because we figured Lisa had enough shit going on to deal with that she didn't need to be burdened with our problems.

"She's okay. It's just going to take her some time to work it all out in her mind."

"I get it." I figured she probably did. No doubt about it, Lisa had been through a lot in her short life, and I bet she spent hours working through it all in her mind.

"Right, let's get your mum some water and then I'll take you to school."

She did as I asked and once I'd made sure Michelle had everything she needed, I took Lisa to school. She seemed more at ease after our conversation, but I made a mental note to mention it to Harlow. Lisa was at that age where I figured she needed a woman looking out for her, and while her mother had improved, it wouldn't hurt for Harlow to keep an eye out. Lisa was far too important to me to allow her to be swallowed by the self-doubt and anxiety the teen years would throw at her.

A couple of hours later, I finally got hold of King, the President of the Sydney Storm chapter.

"Cole, how are you crazy motherfuckers going up there?"

I relaxed back into my chair and put my feet up on the desk. The office of the clubhouse was quiet at ten in the morning with a lot of our guys still sleeping after working security for us at night at our various businesses. "We've got a situation up here with a new asshole in town. Julio Rivera; you know him?"

"Never heard of him. What's he done?" I imagined King leaning forward in his chair the way he did when something intrigued or excited him. 'Situations' excited King and his insane side; he loved nothing more than to get involved if he sensed he could help fuck some shit up.

"Came to town a few months ago from Adelaide and flew under the radar while establishing his drug connections. He wants the big boys out of the way so he can run this State, and in the process, he used Storm to take out some of his competition."

"How the fuck did he do that?"

"That restaurant fire of ours? He organised that and set Ricky up to take the fall. We got rid of Ricky and solved his problem." Anger burned through me just thinking about this asshole. The need to end his agenda consumed me.

"I'll see what the boys know and get back to you."

"Thanks, brother."

"Heard you lost some men. Also heard Griff isn't who we thought he was." I couldn't figure out his tone, but that was King's signature move; he held his cards close to his chest and often left people wondering what he was really thinking.

"The club took a vote and majority ruled on Griff. We're better off without those guys who chose to leave. I stand by the decision to let them walk."

King remained silent for a moment. "A few of them came round here, looking to join."

"And?" I'd suspected that would happen.

"Fuck that shit, brother. I don't want men in my club who can't stand by a majority ruling. I told Hyde to show them the door." He paused before adding, "I'll be completely honest with you, Cole – I've always liked Griff and always suspected there was something more to him. I never saw his truth coming, though, but I couldn't give a fuck about it. His loyalty speaks for itself. You made the right call."

King had a way of surprising the hell out of me. "Yeah." I was thankful for his support, but it wouldn't have bothered me if he hadn't given it. King and I had disagreed in the past, and I'd learnt that he never let a disagreement get between you. So long as you stayed on his good side, you were okay; it was only when he felt wronged that you needed to start getting your affairs in order.

"I'll be in touch," he said and then ended the call.

"You got hold of King?"

I looked up to find Griff in the doorway. Standing, I said, "Yeah, he doesn't know Julio, but he's putting out the feelers."

Griff nodded and then jerked his head in the direction of the bar. "Rogue's here."

"Good. I'm hoping Colt will arrive later today, too."

"You want me to fill Rogue in about what's going on?"

"No, he came over to my place last night and I talked to him already.

We headed out to the bar where Rogue had started drinking for the day already.

Fuck.

"Not much changes with some people," Griff muttered.

"My thoughts exactly," I agreed with him. Rogue had gone nomad just over a year ago after he'd had a falling out with Marcus over his drinking and partying. He'd often let the club down due to the benders he went on, and Marcus had given him an ultimatum to either clean up or clear out.

Rogue eyed me with a grin as I headed his way. "How's that little firecracker of yours today? Still pissed at me?"

"Trust me, you were the last thing on her mind this morning," I muttered. Harlow had been annoyed with him last night and had refused to have anything to do with Rogue after I'd found her on the back deck with him. However, she hadn't even mentioned his name this morning.

"We should have a club get-together tonight, celebrate me and Colt coming home, and you could bring her. She and I should get to know each other better, especially if I'm gonna come back to Brisbane for good."

I raised my brows. "You're thinking of coming back for good?"

"I figure it's time. Now that Marcus isn't around to bust my balls."

Griff grunted next to me as I started to say, "We need to get one thing - " My phone cut me off as I began talking and I ignored it until I realised it was my mother calling; she'd just keep ringing until I answered, so I cut the conversation short to speak with her.

"Hi," I answered the call as I turned away from Rogue.

"Scott," she started and then paused for a moment. Our relationship still hadn't fully recovered after we'd had an almost falling out over Dad before his death. We'd been working on it since, but at times we were still a little hesitant with each other. "I just wanted to check on how Harlow is."

"You know you could call her and ask her yourself."

"I didn't want to harass the poor girl when I know she's still getting over her loss."

I paced on the spot. "Mum, has it ever occurred to you that this could have been the perfect opportunity for you and Harlow to establish a bond?" When Harlow and I had gotten together, my relationship with Mum had been

65

strained, and as a consequence, Mum and Harlow had never had the chance to really get to know each other.

"You're right." Her voice was soft and I heard the thought going on in her head. "I'll call her myself. Might even try to organise some girl time with her. Do you think she'd be interested in that?"

The sight of Colt entering the bar momentarily distracted me and I returned his chin jerk. "I've gotta go, Mum, but yeah, call her and organise that because I'm pretty sure she'd be interested." Hell, I was interested in that because it could mean the end of my mother phoning me every second day or so to check on my woman.

I ended the call and made my way to Colt. We greeted each other with a slap on the back. "Long time, no see, motherfucker," he said with a shit-eating grin on his face.

Returning his grin, I said, "About time you came home, brother." Colt had left two years ago and we'd seen him only once since. He had no family left in Brisbane and I figured the memories he did have kept him away. Couldn't blame the guy; if I'd survived what he had, I wouldn't want to come back either.

He surveyed the bar. "Things have changed around here."

I frowned. "Hardly." No changes had occurred that I was aware of.

His gaze came back to mine, and his face turned serious. "I don't mean the fucking furniture, Scott. I'm talking about the fact Marcus isn't around any longer, and the fact seven of our men have left, which in my opinion was probably the best thing to happen to the club at this point."

"The best thing because?" I needed to know where he stood on this because if I was going to assemble a team of guys ready to support me at any turn, I had to make sure I selected the right ones.

His gaze turned sure, and when he spoke, the truth in his words rang out loud and clear. "If I'm gonna come back here and even think about taking your back, I wanna know that the men by my side support you one hundred fucking percent. When we're out there at war with these assholes and they've got us by the dick, I wanna know I'm standing next to a man who would rather have his dick cut off than give up our club."

"Sounds about right," Griff said as he joined us and caught the last part of the conversation.

Colt turned to Griff. "I hope to fuck I never have to have my dick cut off, but my loyalty runs that deep. Those members that left didn't share the same sense of loyalty as far as I'm concerned or else they'd still be here."

"I'm with you on that," I said.

Colt's seriousness vanished and his grin returned. "You boys up for a ride? Been too long since we've all been out. Thought we could blow off some steam before we get down to business."

A ride hadn't been on my agenda today, but I eyed Griff and said, "Sounds like the best fuckin' idea anyone around here has had for weeks. You in?"

He nodded. "Yeah, brother, I'm in."

We rounded everyone up and ten minutes later, our pipes deafened the neighbourhood.

Best fucking sound in the world.

Chapter Four
Harlow

"It's nearly seven, babe. Do you need to be at work by eight?"

I cracked one eye open and attempted to get my bearings. Scott's legs came into sight as the sunlight streaming through the window hit me. Squeezing my eyes closed again, I grumbled, "Why is it seven already?"

Scott chuckled and the bed dipped as he sat next to me. His hand trailed down my back and then he pressed a kiss to my shoulder. "This is why you've gotta stop doing those shifts at Indigo. You're exhausted."

My eyes blinked open and I rolled onto my back. "I'm not exhausted; I just wish I had more time in bed this morning."

The way his brows pulled together told me he didn't believe me. "When's your next shift at Indigo?"

"Tomorrow night." I sat up and pushed the sheet off me. Swinging my legs off the bed, I stood so I could go to the toilet. Scott, however, moved fast and blocked me.

"I'll take you and pick you up tomorrow; you were in no shape to drive last night."

He was right. He'd arranged with one of his boys to get my car home early in the night so that he could pick me up at the end of my shift, and I'd been so tired when he arrived. Smiling up at him, I nodded. "I agree. Thank you."

"Fuck me, did I just hear that right?" he muttered.

"No need to be a smartass about it." I pushed him gently so I could move past him, and his eyes crinkled into a smile. God, I was a sucker for those crinkles. He could ask me to do anything and I would do it if he flashed them at me.

I showered and got ready for work, and then met him in the kitchen where he had coffee ready for me. Taking it from him, I drank some before saying, "Your mother called me yesterday."

The way he said, "Yeah," made me think he already knew this.

"Did you know she was going to?"

He drank some of his coffee while his gaze moved to mine. "She told me she was going to try and organise to meet up with you."

I leant against the counter and cradled my mug with both hands. "Scott, she was so strange on the phone that I didn't know what to say. I think I must have come across all wrong." Just thinking about it now caused my body to tense up. Making a good impression on his mother rated high on my list of priorities, and I'd been so caught off guard when she rang that I ended up rambling like an idiot.

"Just be you. She's feeling as nervous as you are."

"That's all you're gonna give me?" I stared at him, hoping he'd share at least a little bit more about how I should deal with his mother.

He rinsed his mug and placed it in the dish rack. "I don't know much more than you, Harlow. She's been ringing me to check on you and I suggested to her yesterday it would be a fuck of a lot easier if she just rang you direct. And then she said she'd try to organise girl time with you, or some shit like that."

As he tried to move past me, I put my hand on his arm to halt him. "She's been ringing you? Like, more than once?"

"Yes." He seemed frustrated with me.

"Don't you get like that at me," I warned. "Getting to know your mother is important to me, and I'm going to need your help."

His eyes crinkled again and he dropped a kiss onto my lips before swiping his keys off the counter and saying, "I'll talk to you about this tonight because I've gotta head out now. When are you seeing her?"

"We're having lunch together in a couple of days."

He nodded and slid an arm around my waist. His eyes softened as he asked, "You good today, baby?"

I knew he referred to my rollercoaster emotions. "I'm good," I replied, my voice a little breathy because when Scott did soft, it made me a little breathless. I loved that he didn't give that softness to everyone; he made me feel special.

With one last kiss, he let me go and took a few steps towards the front door before pausing and turning back to face me. "That bossy shit you just pulled on me is hot, sweetheart. I'm loving the fuck out of this new side to you."

I watched him leave; disappointed we both had work today. It would have been the perfect day to stay home in bed together.

Nine hours later, I'd finished another long day at the café and had dropped into the supermarket to grab some meat for dinner when Scott texted me.

Scott: I'm gonna be late tonight. Can you check in on Michelle and Lisa?

Me: Sure. You okay?

Scott: Some club stuff just went down. Will tell you when I get home.

Me: Okay. I'll take care of Michelle. You just concentrate on you and don't worry about us.

He didn't reply after that and concern edged its way into my mind – Scott usually phoned rather than texting. However, I pushed the worry to the side and concentrated on taking care of what he'd asked me to do. I grabbed everything I would need for dinner, as well as the ingredients to make Michelle some soup because I knew from previous experience it was something she would eat, and then headed home.

After dumping everything inside, I made my way next door.

"Hi Harlow," Lisa greeted me after I waited nearly five minutes for her to answer the door, and I realised she was now also sick.

"Hey, honey. You're not feeling well?" I stepped inside, closed the door behind me, and followed her into her bedroom where she slumped onto her bed, curling into a ball.

"My throat is so sore." She could barely get the words out, and my sympathy kicked into gear. Lisa didn't get sick often and she never complained, so for her to be telling me this meant she must be feeling awful.

"You're burning up," I said as I placed my hand on her forehead. "Have you taken some Advil?"

She nodded, but didn't speak again.

"I'm just going to get a washer and I'm also going to check on your mum, okay?"

Again, a nod, but no words.

I left her and found Michelle asleep in her bed. Pressing my hand to her forehead, I found that her fever seemed to have broken. Thank goodness.

A couple of minutes later, I sat with Lisa on her bed and tried to cool her a little with a cold washer. She shifted so that she could curl into my lap, and a little while later she was asleep.

As I sat with her, running my hand gently over her head in an attempt to help her sleep, pain sliced through my heart as I thought about doing this for my own child. I loved Lisa as if she was my own, but after losing my baby, everything felt different. Doing this for Lisa was high on my priorities, however doing it for my own child one day was something I prayed I would get to do.

Lisa fell into a deep sleep, and I tried to leave her a couple of times, but each time she clung to me, clearly not

74

ready for me to leave. Eventually, I fell asleep with her, not waking until Scott touched my shoulder.

"Harlow." His voice broke through my sleep and I blinked my eyes open to find him staring down at me.

I smiled up at him and this time when I moved, Lisa shifted onto her side and continued to sleep. "Hi, you," I whispered as I stood.

He jerked his chin at Lisa. "She sick, too?"

"Yeah, poor baby, her throat is really sore and she has a fever."

His arm slid around my waist and he pulled me close so he could kiss me. "Sorry I'm so late."

As we left Lisa's room, I asked, "What time is it?" The only thing indicating to me how long I'd slept was the crick in my neck.

"It's nearly eleven."

I frowned as concern snaked through me again. "Is everything okay with the club?"

He led me into Michelle's living room and we sat on the couch. "I'm not sure. We've been doing some digging on that drug dealer I mentioned to you the other day, Julio, and I've gotta head down to Adelaide with J and Nash to check out his connections down there."

My heart beat a little faster. "Should I be worried now? I mean, usually you just send the boys to look into stuff while you stay here. What's making you go this time?"

His eyes held mine and I didn't fail to detect the uncertainty clear in them. "I'm not gonna say this is nothing to worry about because I believe it *is* something to be very concerned about. But I don't want you to panic at the same time. Griff and Wilder will be staying in Brisbane, along with Rogue, Colt and Gunnar. Blade will also be around, as will his men, so I'm not worried for your safety. I do need you to be alert, though, sweetheart. Just keep to your usual routine because I've got eyes on all club members' families now and the usual routines are important for that."

I blinked a few times as I took that information in. *Scott will keep us all safe.* "When are you leaving?"

"Tomorrow morning, about five. It'll take us three days to get there, so all up we'll be gone either six or seven days." He watched me closely, obviously waiting for my response.

I wanted to tell him not to go, and to tell him that I needed him home now, more than ever, but I didn't. I simply nodded my understanding. And then I tried to reassure him I would stay safe – I didn't want him spending unnecessary energy worrying over me when he clearly needed to conserve that energy for the club. "I'll keep to my usual routines. Is there anything else you need me to do while you're away?"

"Yes, can you keep an eye on Madison and Velvet? I'm sure they'll be fine, but I want us all to be looking out for each other. I don't want to take any chances on this, not when I don't know enough about this asshole."

"Will do, baby," I promised. "And I'll make sure Michelle and Lisa are okay, too. I think Michelle is getting better – her fever seems to have passed."

He stood. "We should stay here tonight in case either of them need us." Eyeing the couch, he added, "I know it will be uncomfortable, but I don't want to leave them when they're both sick."

Standing next to him, I shook my head in disagreement. "No, you should go home and get a good night's rest. I'll sleep here on the couch."

"The couch is fine for me."

Of course he would argue with me, but I decided to put my foot down on this one; no way did I want Scott to attempt a long ride after a night of shitty sleep. "You need your sleep, Scott. We don't both need to be here. I mean, chances are they won't even wake up."

His brows pulled together the way they did when he was about to argue with me. "Harlow -" he began, but I cut him off.

"No," I said forcefully. "Don't argue with me because I'm not backing down on this. I've told you I'll do what you asked while you're away; the only thing I'm asking is for you to get some sleep tonight." I kept my eyes trained on his, letting him know I had no intention of giving in.

After watching me for a good few moments, he finally caved with a raise of his brows. "Okay, sweetheart, you win. I'll be back just before five to say goodbye." He planted a deep kiss on my lips and then left me to head over to our house.

I gathered up a pillow and blanket, and settled onto the couch for some sleep. My body was weary and I knew it wouldn't take me long to fall asleep, not even on this pain-inducing couch.

My last thoughts as I drifted off were that I could do six days without Scott; of course I could. But they'd be some long days filled with worry, and spent missing him. I'd miss his reassuring presence. On the days I doubted myself, Scott gave me wings, and I hoped the physical distance between us wouldn't change that.

Chapter Five
Harlow

"Baby, wake up."

I attempted to roll over, but the pain shooting through my hip and up along my back caused me to wince and halt my movement. Not a good way to start a day. After a few moments, I tried again, and this time was able to roll over. When I opened my eyes, I found Scott crouching next to the couch I lay on. "Morning," I mumbled, my voice all groggy and my thoughts jumbled as to why I was asleep on Michelle's couch.

"Fuck, I knew I should have stayed here and let you go home," he muttered, his voice sounding as annoyed as his face looked. "Can you move?"

I nodded. "Yes." But even as the word came out, I knew it was a lie, or at least, a partial lie. I could probably move, but it would hurt.

"Bullshit." He called me out, and I simply smiled at him rather than arguing with him about it.

Wincing as I sat, I placed my palm against his cheek. "I love you for caring, baby, but I will be okay. Once I get going and have a shower, the stiffness will ease. How did you sleep?"

The way he paused momentarily told me everything I needed to know; he hadn't slept well. However, he tried to reassure me. "I've had enough sleep." He'd placed his hands on my thighs when I sat, and he now ran them up my legs to my waist. Gripping me there, he said, "Fuck, I need more time with you, but I've gotta go." My disappointment matched his.

I took hold of his face as I nodded. "I know."

Pressing his body into mine, he caught my lips in a kiss. I hated the fact I had morning breath and that this would be the last kiss we'd share for a week, but there was no time to change this, so I kissed him back. He didn't seem to care because he deepened the kiss to the point where he had me panting for more. But again, there was no time for more.

80

When he finally ended the kiss, he growled, "Fuck...I need to fuck you before I go." His eyes were all over me, and his hands moved to slide under my ass. "A week without you is gonna fuckin' kill me."

I knew how he felt – I felt the same way. My hands moved to his belt. "I need you, too." God, how I needed him.

Our hands were a wild tangle of fighting against the clock to get enough clothes off so we could say goodbye in the one way we both needed. Sex was the glue that held us together at the moment in a way that nothing else could. Even when I felt like the words I spoke were all wrong and not useful in moving us back together after I'd held him away, the sex reassured me that we'd be okay.

"Harlow." Lisa's voice cut through the darkness and my body stilled.

Shit.

Scott pulled away from me and quickly did up his pants before standing. Turning to face her, he said, "Hey, darlin', how you feeling?"

He moved towards her as I gathered my thoughts.

"I think I'm going to vomit," she admitted, sounding disoriented from sleep.

Moving fast, he took her to the bathroom and I could hear his soothing voice as he looked after her. Eventually, I stood and stretched my body. The pain had eased a little, allowing me to move without too much trouble.

Knowing that Scott had to leave, I joined them in the bathroom. "You should go," I suggested as his eyes came to mine. "I'll take over with Lisa."

Conflict sat heavy in his eyes. He was clearly torn about leaving. When his phone sounded with a text, he muttered, "Fuck." After checking it he found my gaze again. "I hate leaving you like this, but that was J...I gotta go."

I nodded. "I know," I whispered.

We swapped positions so I could take over with Lisa. His hand settled around my waist for a moment and he kissed me goodbye. God, what a way to say goodbye – standing in the toilet as you waited for a child to vomit. And both of us frustrated by no goodbye sex.

He rested his forehead against mine and remained silent for a beat. When he finally lifted it, he said, "I swear, I'm gonna make this asshole pay for dragging me away from you." His tone made it clear he would follow through on that promise.

I squeezed his hand. "Okay, you should go before I try and stop you from leaving."

He hesitated for another minute and then blew out a long breath. "Yeah," he said gruffly.

After saying goodbye to Lisa, and after giving me one more kiss, he left us. My heart constricted and I wondered again how I would get through the next six or seven days.

You'll be fine and he'll be home soon.

And yet, a sense of foreboding had lodged itself deep in the pit of my stomach.

What if he isn't as invincible as he thinks he is?

I was supposed to work at the café that day and then at Indigo that night. My dilemma over this centred on the fact Lisa and Michelle were both sick. If I'd believed Michelle was well enough to care for Lisa, I would have had no problem leaving them to go to work. But she was far from being well enough to do that.

My saving grace appeared in the most unlikely form.

Scott's mother.

She phoned me a couple of hours after Scott left, to see how I was doing.

"Madison told me that Scott and J left for Adelaide this morning. I'm just calling to see if there is anything I can do to help you while Scott's away," she said.

I sighed as I slumped down into a chair at Michelle's kitchen table. I'd just gotten Lisa back to sleep after giving her more Advil. My weariness caused my tongue to loosen in a way it never had around Sharon. "Can you work some shifts for me at my mum's café and then at Indigo? That's my biggest worry today," I blurted out, not really meaning for her to do what I'd asked – it was more a way for me to get my frustrations out.

She was silent for a moment, probably trying to process my strange request. And then she came through for me. "I've got the day off today. I can help however you need me to, Harlow. What's going on?"

I sat up straight. "Really? That would be awesome, because Lisa and Michelle are really sick and I feel like they need someone to stay and help them. Maybe you could do that while I go to work."

She didn't hesitate. "I can be there in half an hour."

Relief coursed through me. "Thank you so much, Sharon. I really appreciate it."

"I'll see you soon," she promised and hung up, leaving me staring at my phone with a mixture of surprise and gratitude.

"Well, I'll be damned," I murmured before dragging myself off the chair so I could go home and get showered and dressed for work.

Just after half an hour later, Sharon turned up and I let her in as I combed my wet hair.

"You look exhausted, honey," she said as I led her into the kitchen. I'd spent a little bit of time with her since she and Scott had started rebuilding their relationship, but the awkwardness I'd always felt remained. I wished it away, but figured that would just take time.

I finished combing my hair and gave her my full attention. "I do feel really tired. I've been working a lot of double shifts lately because Indigo is short-staffed and need me."

She turned thoughtful. "You know, I could take on some of those shifts for you, if you want."

I stared at her. She could definitely do those shifts because she knew everything about working a bar after Layla had trained her. "That would be great. I'll mention it to Wilder today and get him to contact you to see which ones match up with your schedule." Why had I not thought of this already?

Her face spread into a smile as if I'd made her day. "Okay, I'm glad we got that sorted. Scott would never have asked me; he doesn't like to involve me with the club much any more." Sadness weaved its way through her words and touched me. I'd noticed that about Scott also.

A flash of boldness overtook me and I acknowledged the elephant in the room. "Sharon, why have we never taken the time to get to know one another?"

Uncertainty filled her features and she hesitated with her reply. "That's on me, Harlow. I know you tried to reach out to me a few times over the last year, but for one reason or another, I was reluctant to get close. My relationship with Scott went to virtually non-existent while I was still living in denial over Marcus, so I kept myself away. Probably because deep down I knew Scott wanted to push me into facing who his father really was, and I wasn't ready to face that. And now after Marcus's death, I've struggled to find myself. It's stupid, really, because you'd think his death would be the perfect opportunity for me to start over, but change and me don't do well together." Her honesty and willingness to be vulnerable inspired me to lay myself out there for her, too.

"I've learnt that finding yourself is hard work," I said softly. "It's like this never-ending struggle with doubt, and fear, and hope. And it's like a rollercoaster ride of feeling good about yourself one day and then down the next. God, some days I can be up and down five times in one freaking hour. Drives me insane."

She smiled and nodded. "Yeah, I know that feeling all too well."

I cocked my head, feeling reflective, and glad to be having this discussion. Not everyone liked to admit their struggles; I always felt relief whenever someone opened themselves up like this. "Why do we do it to ourselves?"

She sighed. "I have no idea. And you'd think that by my age I should, but I'm beginning to wonder if I'll ever get to a point where I've got all this shit about myself figured out."

"Let's start over," I suggested.

"You and me, you mean?"

"Yes. Let's put everything that has happened over the last twelve months behind us and start afresh. I want you in our lives, and so does Scott."

Her face creased in a frown. "I think Scott and I have a lot of work ahead of us before he'll let me back in fully. But I'm happy that you and I can get to know each other now."

"Scott's a moody bastard, you know that. Take my word for it – he might not tell you or show you very well, but he wants you in his life. He might need some gentle encouragement, though, to acknowledge it." I gave her a huge smile and then added, "I'm so glad we got to have this conversation today. I've been a little nervous about our lunch date."

The tense set of her shoulders disappeared and she returned my smile. "Me too. Now, tell me what you need me to do today."

I filled her in on Lisa and Michelle, and took her over to their house. They were both sleeping, so I woke Michelle up to let her know what was happening. She was so ill that she only nodded her agreement and then fell straight back asleep.

After I made sure Sharon had everything she needed, I headed back home to finish getting ready for work, and then drove to the café while ignoring the tickle in my throat. I had no time to be sick.

"I spoke with Sharon," Wilder said to me that night after I arrived at Indigo for my shift. I'd told him that morning to call her. "She's gonna pick up some of your shifts at Indigo."

"Thank God."

He narrowed his eyes at me. "Are you coming down with something?"

"No, I'm just tired, that's all." I followed him into the office and asked, "Have you heard from Scott or any of the boys?"

"No. You?"

I shook my head. "No." I'd tried not to think about them all day, but it had been a futile attempt. I'd also struggled to think about anything else besides Lisa and her mother.

Wilder stopped what he was doing and came to me. "Harlow, you don't need to worry about Scott. He's got this shit covered." Wilder was a good guy and the way he spoke to me, with care, just reinforced what I already knew.

"I know you're trying to reassure me and I appreciate it, and I'm trying not to worry, but it's just my nature to always think about those I love. I have faith that he'll be okay, though."

His gaze held mine for another few moments and then he nodded. "I'll let you know when I hear something, but my bet's on him calling you before he calls us."

Smiling at him, I said, "Thank you." Taking a step backwards and out of the office, I added, "I better go get ready for my shift."

88

"I've gotta head out soon, but I've got Rogue stationed out front keeping an eye on security. Just let him know if anything strange happens, yeah?"

"Will do," I agreed before leaving him to head to the staff room.

I ran into Rogue in the hallway, not loving the way his gaze zoomed in on my chest. "Hi, gorgeous," he greeted me. His voice grated on me as much as his gaze did.

Fixing an icy glare on him, I said, "Don't call me gorgeous. And I don't appreciate your eyes on my chest."

He raised his brows. "You're fuckin' kidding me, aren't you?"

"No, I'm not fucking kidding you," I snapped, my irritation jumping to record levels. It took a lot to piss me off, but this guy had managed to do it both times we'd come in contact.

Anger clouded his features. "If I want my eyes on your tits, that's exactly where I'm gonna have my fuckin' eyes. I don't appreciate club whores telling me what the fuck I can and can't do."

My blood boiled to the point where I thought it could blister my skin. "You need to get your facts straight, asshole, because I don't appreciate club members calling me a whore when that is so far from what the hell I am."

His hand shot out and he gripped my bicep as he shoved me against the wall. Bending his face to mine, he snarled, "Bitch, I really don't give a flying fuck what you are. Stay out of my way if you don't want my eyes on your tits and my hands on your body."

My heart beat faster and my breaths grew shallow, but I'd be damned if I would let him threaten me like this. Shoving him hard so he stumbled back, I warned, "Don't ever place your hands on me again. I can guarantee you that you won't like the repercussions if you do."

The way he sneered sent chills along my spine and I fought not to wrap my arms around my body in an attempt to shelter myself from him. I refused to give him the satisfaction of that.

He opened his mouth to speak again, but at that minute, Wilder came our way. "Everything okay with you two?" he enquired, a frown on his face.

Rogue flashed a huge smile at him and nodded. "We were just getting acquainted. Everything's good here. You going home, man?"

Wilder stared at Rogue for a moment before turning his attention to me. "You good, Harlow?"

I regained control over my breathing and nodded. "I'm good. And I just had a call from Scott who asked me to let you know he wants Rogue stationed over at Trilogy tonight. He's called Blade to send someone else here for the night."

Wilder's face pulled into a frown. "Really? He hasn't called me about that."

I watched Rogue carefully, taking in the way his face contorted in anger. *Fuck you, asshole.* Holding his gaze, I nodded and said, "Yeah, he said he didn't have time to make two calls and - " I turned my gaze to Wilder and hit him with a sweet smile, " – I guess you were right when you hedged your bet that he'd call me first."

Wilder grinned. *Bingo. Way to a man's heart – tell them they were right about something.* "I knew he would, babe." Looking at Rogue, he said, "Okay, brother, I guess you're off strip club duty. I'll catch you later."

Once Wilder had walked away, Rogue got in my face. "What's your fuckin' game, bitch?"

I squared my shoulders. "You wanna fuck with me, expect me to fuck back with you. I'm no club whore; I'm the President's old lady, and I roll over for no one, asshole." I spat my words out before turning on my heel and stalking away from him. My heart had begun beating a million times faster than it usually did; well, at least that was how it felt in my chest. Threatening a man like Rogue wasn't something I had ever done, but as far as I was concerned, it had to be done. I had to show him I wouldn't be a pushover.

As soon as I was safely in the staff room with the door locked behind me, I called Blade.

"Harlow, what's up?" He answered on the second ring.

"Blade, can you spare me a guy tonight? For security at Indigo. Our guy can't make it now."

Without hesitation, he replied, "Consider it done."

I let out the breath I'd been holding in. "Thank you."

"I'll have someone there within half an hour."

91

We ended the call and I relaxed back against the door as my breathing evened out. Now all I had to do was figure out how to keep Rogue away from me while Scott was away. I refused to burden my man with anything else so there was no way I'd share with him what had happened today. Not until he got home, at least.

Chapter Six
Harlow

Knives slicing my throat.

That's what it felt like the next morning when I woke up. Rolling over in bed, I almost cried in agony as I swallowed. By the time I'd made it into the bathroom and grabbed painkillers from the cupboard, my whole body had alerted me to the fact it was also in a great deal of pain. Every muscle ached, and I could have sworn that every bone did, too.

Once I'd taken the pills, I pulled out my phone and texted Sharon who had stayed overnight next door.

Me: You okay? And how's Lisa and Michelle?

Sharon: I'm good. Michelle is doing better today but Lisa is still sick. I'm going to go home and shower and have some sleep in my own bed before coming back to check on them. How are you?

Me: I have their cold now.

Sharon: Are you working today at the café?

Me: Yeah.

Sharon: Sorry honey. I've got your Indigo shift covered tonight so at least you can rest then. I'll check in on you before I leave for work.

Me: Thank you xx

I wanted to call in sick to my mum, but I knew we'd be having a busy day today and that she had no one else to call on, so I got dressed and headed into work.

She took one look at me when I arrived and said, "Go home, baby, I can manage on my own."

"No, you need me today, Mum." I grimaced as I spoke and she shook her head at me.

"I'll manage on my own." She attempted to shoo me away, but I resisted.

Standing my ground, I said, "I'll get better as the day goes on; that's what always happens when I have a cold." The heaviness in my head led me to believe this might not be true today, but no way would I let her know that.

She frowned at me until something caught her eye behind me. When the door bell sounded, I turned to find Madison entering the café with a smile on her face.

"Morning, ladies," she greeted us.

Mum returned her smile. "Madison, will you tell Harlow she is too sick to work today?"

Madison's smile disappeared as her gaze zeroed in on me. "Oh, no! Are you sick, too? So many people are coming down with this cold. Apparently it's a nasty one. You should definitely go home and sleep it off."

"I'll be okay, and honestly, if it gets worse later, I promise I will go home."

Mum sighed; she knew how stubborn I could be. "Fine, but I'm holding you to that." She eyed Madison. "Do you want your usual?"

"I'll make it, Mum. You go do your stuff out the back," I said as I made my way behind the counter.

She muttered something under her breath as she left us to go and get the kitchen ready for the day. I began making Madison's coffee as I asked, "Did you hear from J?"

After settling herself on the stool at the counter, she nodded. "Yeah. And you heard from Scott?"

"I did, but I was at work at Indigo when he rang so I didn't get to talk to him for long." Every word I spoke sliced more pain through my throat and I wondered how I was going to make it through the day.

95

"They're going to be exhausted by the time they get to Adelaide," she said. "I hate it when they do these long rides."

"This is the first really long one Scott has done since we've been together so it's all new to me. I've gotta agree with you – I'm not liking it so far. And especially now that I'm sick, I'm hating it more."

"Do you want me to come and stay with you while you're sick?"

I looked up from what I was doing and gave her a smile. "Your mum is looking out for me, so I'm good, but thank you."

Her eyes widened. "Mum? How? Tell me more!" It was as if she couldn't get her words out fast enough, and I would have laughed if it didn't hurt so much.

"Long story that I will tell you when my throat is better, but she and I are getting to know each other and she's helping me out while Scott's away." I finished making her coffee and passed it to her.

"Thanks," she said as she took her drink. "This is great, Harlow. I'm so happy for you two. And God, this might finally pull Scott into line where Mum's concerned."

A laugh escaped before I could stifle it, and I almost choked when I began coughing. *Oh, God, make the pain go away.*

Mum rushed out from the kitchen with a glass of water for me. As she passed it to me, she said in her firm tone that told me she wouldn't be backing down, "You are going home to bed, Harlow Anne. Don't even try to argue with me."

I held up my hand in surrender and nodded. "I'm going," I promised.

Madison finished her coffee and after I'd assured Mum that I would call her if I needed her, Madison walked me out to my car. The sight of a Storm member sitting on his bike a little way down the road reminded me of Scott, and I missed him a little more. I just wanted to go home and have him wrap me in his arms.

"What are you thinking?"

I found Madison watching me thoughtfully. "Just that I miss Scott. I know it's silly because he'll be home soon, but we've never been apart; I think that's why I'm missing him so much."

"And probably because you're sick, too. When I'm sick, all I want is J."

"Yeah..." I squeezed my eyes shut as I coughed. The pain was almost unbearable now so I said my goodbyes and drove home as fast as I could. Sleep and medicine were the only two things on my mind. The sooner I got them, the sooner I could start getting better. And I needed to get better fast because I wanted to take care of things while Scott was away.

What is that noise?

Make it stop.

I fumbled in the dark at the place I thought the noise was coming from. It needed to stop. The pounding in my head was only getting worse the longer the noise continued.

The more I fumbled, the more frustrated I grew until eventually my brain shifted into gear and I realised it was my phone ringing. Shifting onto my side, I opened my eyes to locate it.

"Hello?" I croaked into the phone.

God, it's so dark.

How long have I been asleep for?

"You sound awful, baby."

Scott.

My heart soared even as my pain kicked up another notch.

"I *feel* awful," I whinged. "Can you just do all the talking, 'cause it hurts to speak?"

He didn't say anything for a moment and then – "Fuck, Harlow, I'm sorry I'm not there for you." His regret rang loud in his tone.

"No, don't be sorry, I'm okay. It's just a cold and I'm a whinger." I rallied every ounce of positivity I could muster in the hope he would worry less over me. "And besides, your mum is looking out for me. How's your trip?"

"If there's one thing I'm sure of it's that you're not a whinger, so don't try and give me that bullshit that you're fine when I know you're not. I'm gonna send one of the boys over to look out for you."

Shit.

No.

I sat up straight in the bed to gather myself for this conversation now. If he intended to send Rogue over, this could get messy, and messy was the last thing I wanted for Scott now. Not when he needed to concentrate on what he was doing in Adelaide.

"No, Scott, please don't send anyone over. Your mum and Madison are all I need, and they're here for me. I'll be very upset if you pull one of the boys off Storm work when I know you need all hands on deck." God, it hurt my throat to say all those words. I just prayed he would listen to me.

Silence.

I waited.

He blew out a breath. "If you get worse, I'm sending someone. And you won't argue," he stated forcefully and I knew to let it go. I wouldn't get worse and if I did, I wouldn't let on.

Time to change the subject. "So you guys are doing okay on the road?"

"Don't think I don't know what you're doing there, Harlow," he said in his bossy voice, "And yes, we're making good time. We'll be in Adelaide sometime tomorrow morning."

I ignored his bossy ways. "Good. I'm happy to hear that." And relieved.

A knock on my front door distracted me so I missed what he said next. When he said – "Harlow?" – I shifted my attention back to him.

"Sorry, there's someone at the front door. It's probably your mum." I moved off the bed to pad out to the door.

"I'll let you go, sweetheart. You ring me if you need anything and I'll make sure you have it."

I smiled at the love I heard in his voice. "I will. And ring me when you get to Adelaide so I know you're safe."

We ended the call just as I pulled the door open.

I frowned.

I hadn't been expecting to open the door to that.

"Hello, officers."

"Good evening, Miss. We're looking for Scott Cole. Is he home?" Out of the two officers standing in front of me, the one who spoke looked like the nice one. The other dude looked to be the asshole.

"No, he's away this week. Can I help at all?"

The asshole spoke next and ignored my question completely. "When is he back?"

"I'm not sure exactly. If you leave me your card, I'll pass it on when he returns." He had to be dreaming if he thought I'd give up any information about Scott.

His jaw clenched. "I wouldn't advise you to withhold information from us, Harlow. This is a serious matter we're investigating."

He knows my name.

I shouldn't have been surprised. Scott had told me that Storm was often visited by the cops; I'd just never witnessed it. And I figured my ties to the club President would warrant them looking into me.

Holding my chin up, I said, "I'm not withholding information. I honestly do not know when he will be back because it depends on how his business goes. I will, however, be sure to mention to him that you stopped by. Now, gentlemen, I am sick and want to go back to bed, so if there's nothing further, I'm going to say goodnight."

Asshole raised his brows, but remained silent. The other one nodded once. "Be sure to tell Scott we're looking for him."

I watched as they walked down the stairs and saw Sharon walking up them at the same time. She scowled at the cops as she passed them.

After I'd closed the door behind her, she turned and asked, "What did those pricks want?"

I shrugged. "They were after Scott, but I'm not sure why."

She drew a long breath and as she blew it out, her shoulders slumped while her face turned white. "Fuck," she muttered, and made her way to the kitchen table.

Following her, I asked, "Why do you look like you're about to vomit?" Her stress fed mine, and I needed to know what was going on.

We sat at the table, and she fidgeted while avoiding eye contact so I pushed her. "Sharon, what the hell is going on?"

Her eyes snapped to mine and my heart fell into my stomach at the fear I saw there. Something bad had happened.

"Have you ever questioned absolutely everything in your life, Harlow?" Her voice was almost a whisper and I could sense the demons she was wrestling with. I didn't know exactly which demons she was referring to, but the air between us sat heavy with introspection, and with that always came demons.

"Yes, I have. Recently, in fact."

She nodded slowly, taking that in. Turning it over in her mind. And then she continued. "I've made a lot of bad choices in my life, but the one right thing I did will be the thing that comes back to haunt me forever." She stared at me and I stilled. The ghost of her past had her in its grips and I knew she was about to bare her soul to me, and I wasn't sure I wanted her to. We hardly knew each other, and I had no comprehension of the life she'd led because the Storm she knew and the Storm I knew were almost completely different. She'd lived through the years where they dealt in crime and filth, whereas that had all been cleaned up by the time I came along. I wouldn't know how to help her in her hour of confession.

I waited silently for her to speak.

And when she did, she stunned me completely.

"I was involved in my husband's death and I think the police have worked it out. They came to my house today, too. Asked me a lot of questions before I refused to answer any more."

I stared at her while my heart rate picked up speed.

"I thought Scott killed him," I eventually blurted while still trying to wrap my mind around what she'd just said.

Her eyes widened. "No. It was me - " She stopped suddenly and I wondered what else she had been about to say, but I didn't ask because I really didn't want to know.

Unsure of what else to say to her, I went with – "I wouldn't blame you for killing Marcus." When she just sat staring at me in silence, I added, "I mean, he was an awful man." Oh God, was I putting my foot in it now? She'd been married to the man for years and I'd just labelled him as awful.

"You must wonder why I stayed married to him for all those years." She spoke quietly again. I was sure I could sense shame woven through her words.

I shook my head. "It's not my place to wonder things like that, Sharon. That was your business...your life. No one else's."

"God, Scott is right about you."

My brows pulled together in a frown. "In what way?"

"He told me he loves you because you have this amazing capacity to see the good in people even when there is no good to be seen." She took a deep breath before continuing. "I thought I was a strong woman by staying with him. I convinced myself that staying was the right thing to do for the kids; I didn't want them to have a broken family. And I convinced myself I loved him. In the end, I broke all of us." Her shoulders drooped and the mask she always wore slipped. In its place sat a cracked veneer of regret and self-loathing.

Oh my goodness.

My heart broke for her.

I reached for her hand and held it. "Sharon, everyone's definition of strong is different depending on the life experiences we've each had. You were strong in the only way you knew how, and you protected your children through it all. You have to give yourself credit for that. As far as me wondering about your marriage, I never judge another woman's choice in a man because I'm not the one walking in their shoes. I can never know what has happened to them in their life that they feel compelled to make that choice. Someone with family support and self belief possibly wouldn't stand for domestic violence or cheating, but a lot of women don't have that, or don't feel they have that. The rest of the world needs to stop judging women for the resources they don't have. It would be a nicer world if instead of judging, we helped. And I sure as hell will never know the intricacies of any relationship because the only people who will ever understand that are the two people involved." It hurt my throat so much to say all this, but it was important to me for her to hear what I wanted to say so I pushed through it.

She squeezed my hand as tears fell down her cheeks. "Thank you," she whispered.

I passed the tissue box sitting on the table to her. "You don't need to thank me for something that should be a given in life. But I want you to know that I am here for you. I'm not sure if I have much to offer you, but I've always got a shoulder and a listening ear."

She smiled through her tears. "I'm sorry to dump all this on you when you're so sick. I ran out of friends over the years; they all deserted me when they couldn't stand Marcus."

I swallowed back the tears her words induced. "They weren't your real friends, then."

Her gaze zeroed in on the way my face contorted as pain stabbed at my throat. Standing, she announced, "I'm going to go so that you can go back to bed and sleep off that pain. Do you need me to do anything for you before I go?"

I shook my head as I stood next to her. "No, I've got painkillers and tissues; that's all I need. I'm going to dose up and go back to sleep." I wanted to ask her more about the police, but my pain was so extreme and tiredness had washed over me again so I left it for now.

Tomorrow. I'd be better tomorrow and I'd follow it up then.

Surely she was wrong.

Surely the police were looking into something else.

Chapter Seven
Scott

I splashed water on my face and stared in the mirror of the clubhouse bathroom. We'd arrived in Adelaide a couple of hours ago and at the clubhouse about fifteen minutes ago. Tired eyes stared back at me. The trip had been exhausting and my body craved rest, but we had shit to take care of. There would be no rest. Not now, and not until we'd taken care of Julio once and for all. Patience and I were developing a relationship, but it wasn't one I wanted to pursue. With each passing day, my restlessness grew. I needed Julio dealt with, and yet, we had to make sure we did it right. His connections ran deep and the last thing Storm needed was a pissed off connection.

"Scott, you ready, brother?"

I turned to face J and nodded. "Let's do this."

He returned my nod and we headed out to the main area of the clubhouse where Bourne waited for us.

Bourne's eyes met mine as we entered and I struggled to figure out what lay behind them. In his forty years, he'd clearly perfected the art of hiding his thoughts and emotions.

"To what do I owe the pleasure of Scott Cole visiting me?" he asked as we approached.

I didn't have the time to beat around the bush, nor the inclination. "Can we speak in private?"

His eyes narrowed at me before he nodded. I left Nash and J with the Adelaide members and followed Bourne into his office. After he'd shut the door behind him, he crossed his arms over his chest and said, "Spit it out."

Not much ever changed with this man – he wore grumpy like a second skin and always had. At least he was predictable in that respect. In other ways, he had to be one of the most unpredictable men I knew. "Julio Rivera. You know him?" I watched carefully for any level of recognition in his eyes.

He nodded once. "Yep. He owns the drugs in this state. I'm not a fan of the man."

"You've got an agreement with him?"

"I do. But I don't like it."

"Why?"

"Why the fuck do you think?" He unfolded his arms and pulled out his phone. After scrolling through it and finding what he was after, he said, "I want the asshole gone so Storm can have his territories."

"You're looking to expand?" It wouldn't surprise me – he'd always had a God complex.

"I want the entire State."

Of course he fucking did. I raked my fingers through my hair. "How the hell are you planning to do that? From what I know, Julio has a strong hold on it and everyone in it."

He watched me like a lion watched its prey. "I figure you and I are gonna work on that together."

My brows pulled together. "How the fuck do you figure that?"

He placed his phone in his palm and played me a recording of two people discussing the fire at our restaurant, Trilogy. In particular, they were discussing the fact they were responsible for the fire and what they had hoped to achieve by setting it – Storm getting rid of Ricky Grecian. When the recording finished, he eyed me and shared, "That was Julio and his right hand man."

I stood in silence while I processed what he'd just shared with me. "How did you get that recording?"

"Does that matter?"

"As far as I'm concerned, it does. You're indicating your desire for me to work with you to take Julio down –

I'm hardly gonna get into bed with someone unless I know their information is right." I'd never trusted Bourne, and I struggled to trust him now.

He scowled and threw his phone on the table. "Jesus Christ, Cole, you're just how your father described you - a fucking pussy who refuses to take an opportunity when it presents itself."

My body tensed as anger heated me. "See, that's where my father went wrong in life. He didn't pay enough attention to the details. The devil's in the fuckin' details, Bourne. Call me whatever the fuck you want, but I'm not taking your word for anything. You give me what I need and we'll go from there."

Shaking his head at me, he muttered, "Fuck." He then settled against his desk and folded his arms across his chest. "I planted a guy in Julio's crew and he's been feeding me the information I need. If you want to talk to him to verify that, I'll line up a meet. He can give you whatever information you want on Julio."

"Line it up for today. I'm heading home tomorrow."

He raised his brows. "You rode all this way, gave up almost a week of your time, just to talk to me and this guy? You couldn't do it over the phone or send someone else?"

"Never can be too sure, Bourne. I needed to see you myself."

He pushed off the desk. "I'll let you know what time."

As I watched him walk out of the office, I knew this was his signal that we were done until later. Suited me. The less time in his presence, the better.

"Hey, baby," Harlow greeted me when I rang her a little while after seeing Bourne. Even though she sounded happy to hear from me, I could discern the act she was putting on for me.

"On a scale of one to ten, how bad do you feel? One being like death," I said as I fidgeted with the diner menu in front of me. We'd left the clubhouse in search of food and found what we needed about half an hour away in a tiny diner off the highway. J and Nash were ordering our food while I rang Harlow.

I heard her sigh through the phone. "Honestly, I'd say I'm at a five today. My throat isn't as bad as it was yesterday; I can at least swallow without feeling like I have a packet of razors going down."

So, she's probably a three or a four.

"Has Mum checked on you today?"

"It's only ten in the morning, Scott. She worked late last night so I wouldn't expect her until this afternoon."

"What about Madison?"

"She rang me and I told her I was doing okay. And before you ask, I've taken the morning off work and if I feel better this afternoon, I'll go in and help Mum then."

"We're leaving Adelaide tomorrow and we'll be as fast as we can."

"Please don't rush back just for me."

"I'll have what I need by tomorrow, sweetheart. By the way, how are Lisa and Michelle?"

"Michelle is much better and Lisa is getting there. I went over and checked on them this morning. How are you feeling?"

I rubbed the back of my neck. "Like shit, but that's to be expected. Nothing a good night's sleep next to you won't fix in a few days." I eyed Nash heading my way with breakfast. "You good if I go? Nash just ordered food."

"Yes, go eat. I'll talk to you later."

"Tonight, baby," I said, and ended the call as Nash placed breakfast on the table.

"Harlow good?" he asked as he slid into the seat across from me.

"No, she's still sick, but trying to tell me she's okay."

I pulled up the contacts on my phone and dialled a number.

Shoving bacon in my mouth, I waited for him to answer. He took his time to answer, finally picking up on about the sixth ring. "Scott, what's up, man?"

"I've got one of the prospects watching Harlow, but I need you to head over to my house and keep an eye on her instead. She's not well and I'm concerned she might pass out or some shit. You good to do that?"

"Sure. Gimme five and then I'm on my way."

112

"Thanks."

"No worries. Anything to help the club."

"Oh, and Rogue, don't let her try and tell you she's okay. I don't want your attention on anything other than Harlow today."

"You got it, man. My day is dedicated to her."

As I placed my phone on the table, it buzzed with a text.

Bourne: Meet is scheduled for one this afternoon. At the clubhouse.

Me: See you then.

"I don't know whether to trust that asshole or not," I muttered after I sent my text. As I met Nash's gaze, I added, "I'm trying to figure out his angle here."

"He obviously wants us to help him take down Julio, but I don't see how having us along for the ride will really help him," Nash said.

"That's what I'm getting stuck on, too."

"Let's check out Julio's crew as best we can before we meet Bourne's guy this afternoon, and then go from there. If we don't trust him, we walk away."

He was right, and I couldn't help but think that any man who'd been aligned with my father was not a man I could trust.

★★★

I walked into the Adelaide clubhouse with trepidation that afternoon. The beady-eyed guy Bourne had with him only raised my levels of concern. Short, almost bald and sweaty as if he had shit to hide, Alex was your typical drug dealing scum.

After Bourne completed the introductions, I said, "I would have thought Julio would have measures in place to weed out traitors. How have you managed to go undetected?"

"I made myself indispensable to him from before he even took me on. Bourne and I planned it way in advance. We were smart about that shit, man, and Julio never suspected a thing. Even when he dug into my background, he couldn't find anything, because Bourne and I had covered it and replaced it with what Julio would accept." His eyes betrayed nothing when I'd expected them to show me he was lying. I'd met enough lying assholes in my life to know the signs and this guy showed none of them.

"So what's your role in Julio's organisation?" J asked. The tense set of his shoulders revealed his hesitation to believe Alex, too.

"I take care of a lot of the shipments and pretty much do anything else he asks me to do. I've brought in a lot of contacts for him; that's how I worked my way up fairly quickly."

"You gave him those contacts?" I looked at Bourne in surprise. "Would have thought you'd wanna keep them for yourself."

Bourne tapped his head. "Being smart's what got me to where I am today, brother. You've gotta be willing to make sacrifices in order to give your enemy a little of what he needs, so that in the long run, he gives you what you need. And even better if he doesn't know it's you giving it to him."

Nash stepped forward, his eyes narrowed on Bourne. "So let me get this straight – through Alex, you've been feeding Julio contacts and learning everything about his business. How do you see that playing out? And how the fuck do we figure into that? And why would we even want to?"

Bourne met Nash's gaze and held it. "I can't make a move on his territory while he's still alive. He's got too much on people that he's bought their loyalty. I also can't kill him because the retaliation will come hard and fast from his people. However, someone else can kill him and while his people scramble to figure out who, I can cause some serious issues for them. The interruption to their business and the uncertainty of it would give me enough scope to make my move." He turned his gaze to me. "That's where you come in."

"You want us to deal with him for you? So *you* can get what you want?" I said.

"You'd be doing yourself a favour, too, Cole. You don't want to live in a state run by Julio. He'll cause you no end of trouble."

"Tell me about that. What trouble could he possibly cause us?" I didn't let on that I already knew what kind of trouble Julio could cause us. I wanted to see how much Bourne would be willing to share.

"I'd think the Trilogy fire was a good example of the shit he gets up to. He also likes to play with his enemies by causing problems between them and their business associates, so for example your wholesalers, that kind of thing. Julio finds ways to make sure everyone needs him, and if he can't do that, he finds ways to make sure you don't fuck with him. He blackmailed me when he got proof of something I did five years ago. Trust me, if you've got skeletons in your closet, he'll find them and use them."

"Say we come on board, what's the plan?" Nash asked.

"Julio has met a woman and from what Alex can figure, she's his weakness. He's planning a weekend away with her soon. We think that's our best time to attack because each time he's taken her away, he only takes a few men with him."

I rubbed the back of my neck. A headache had settled in. "Leave all this with us. We'll take it back to the club and let you know what we decide."

Bourne's jaw clenched. "Don't take too long, brother. This needs to be dealt with as soon as possible. Before Julio makes any more ground in Queensland."

I scowled. "We'll take as fuckin' long as we take, Bourne. I need to be sure this serves us and not just you." My hands clenched by my side as I walked out of the meeting; the desire to tell him what I thought of him sat heavy in my gut, but I kept my mouth shut. I had to be smart about how I handled him. And I had to remember that even though he'd shared information with us, that didn't mean we had or would ever have an alliance with him. Bourne was not the kind of man to form a working relationship with. He'd save your back one day only to turn around and stab you in it the next.

Chapter Eight
Harlow

I eyed the bike behind me as I drove to the clubhouse.

Rogue.

I'd almost choked on a cough when he'd knocked on my door this morning and announced that Scott had sent him to watch over me for the entire day. And the way he'd dropped his gaze to my chest as he'd uttered the words 'watch over you' had almost made me gag.

There'd been no way I was staying at home after he'd arrived there, so I'd made him stay outside while I got dressed, and then I'd decided to head to the clubhouse. I had cake to drop off for the guys before I went to work.

Wilder sat in the clubhouse bar when I arrived, and jerked his chin when he saw me. "You got a minute, Harlow?" he asked as he downed the remainder of his beer.

"Sure," I said before sliding into the chair across from him. I was grateful to be in the company of another club member, and ignored the scowl Rogue gave me.

Wilder hit me with a smile, and I couldn't help but take in how good-looking he was. His dark hair sat slightly messed against his tanned skin while just enough scruff on his face defined his jaw and guaranteed to turn the eye of every woman he walked past. But it was his piercing green eyes that always got me; he used those eyes to convince women to do anything he wanted, and I was no different. He had this way of making you feel good when you said yes to his request, and I'd seen numerous girls fall for his charm.

"How are you feeling? Better?"

"A little better. Why? What are you going to ask me for today?" I gave him a smile to let him know I was okay with him asking me for something.

His smile morphed into a grin. "You know me so well, Harlow." Leaning forward, he continued, "Trilogy reopens in a few days and I desperately need staff. I was doing okay until this morning when a handful of staff quit to go and work at another restaurant. The asshole tried to

119

poach more of our staff but thank fuck they didn't all leave. I'm gonna need to borrow some of the Indigo team for Trilogy, so do you think you'll be well enough to fill in until I train new people?"

And there were those eyes, begging me to say yes.

I nodded. "Of course. Whatever you need, I'm yours."

"Wilder!" A yell cut through the air and we both turned to see where it was coming from.

Gunnar, the newly patched member, stood in the doorway of the bar, staring at Wilder, waiting for his response.

Wilder pushed back his chair and stood. "What?"

"There's a bitch outside looking for a fight. Griff's not around; you wanna take this one or do you want me to deal with her?"

"Fuck," Wilder muttered, "I'll do it." He began stalking out and I quickly followed him. I didn't like to involve myself in club business, but if it was a woman, he might be thankful for my presence.

Rogue sneered at me as I walked past him. "This ain't got nothing to do with you, bitch."

I sent him a glare as I continued on my way. "Screw you, asshole."

"Fuck, I got no clue what Cole sees in you, apart from your tits and ass." He followed close behind and I did my best to ignore him. I had him pegged for the kind of man who loved to get a woman all worked up and then toy with them, and I refused to give him the satisfaction of that.

I stepped outside and recognised the dark-haired woman from the other day – the one who'd been arguing with Scott when I'd brought him cake.

Her angry eyes came to me and then shifted to Wilder who stood in front of me. "So, I need that money back I gave you the other day. Turns out my brother got his drugs from someone else and they're still threatening him over non-payment."

Wilder squared his shoulders. "I don't know anything about any money you gave us." Gone was any trace of the fun and easy-going Wilder, and in his place was a man I wouldn't want to have problems with. His tone made it clear he wasn't interested in discussing this any further.

She crossed her arms over her chest and rested most of her weight on one leg as if she was settling in until she got what she came for. "I gave the dude with the lips the cash. Go ask him for it."

The dude with the lips?

"Babe, he's not here and won't be back for a few days at least, so I suggest you come back then and speak to him yourself."

Scott does have good lips; I would agree with her there. Kissable lips.

"No, *I* suggest you call him and get it for me. Dealing with asshole drug dealers is not the way I wanna spend my time 'til your dude gets back."

I had to give her credit for her perseverance.

Wilder's back muscles shifted under his fitted t-shirt as he shoved his fingers through his hair. She was clearly irritating him, but he held his cool. "I've got a shitload of things to get through today and hassling Scott for your cash isn't one of them, but I can see you're not planning on moving that ass of yours until I do." He pulled his phone out of his back pocket and stabbed at it.

I stepped next to him while he waited for Scott to answer. His annoyance was painted on his face and I watched as he directed his frustrated gaze at the woman. When Scott didn't take the call, he left a message and hung up. "Not much more I can do until he calls me back. Give me your number and I'll let you know when that happens."

She stared at him for a few more moments and I thought she wasn't going to let this go, but then she snapped at him. "Fucking hell! You're not the only one who has shit to do. I've got a million things to do today, one of them being to pay those assholes off before they hurt my brother, and in amongst all this shit, I've gotta deal with the fact I don't have a car to get me where I've gotta go." As she exhaled a long, shitty breath, she rummaged around in her bag.

"I could help," I blurted. When Wilder's head snapped around to face me, I almost wished I hadn't opened my mouth; the glare he directed at me was pure annoyance mixed with a little anger.

"No, you can't, Harlow. Scott will fuckin' kill me if I involve you in this." He threw a don't-argue-with-me look my way, and I did my best to ignore it.

"Look, you don't have time to wait around for Scott so I could do that." I turned my attention to the woman. "And I have a car so I could drive you where you have to go. I just need to be at work in a few hours."

She stared at me like I had two heads. "You serious?"

"Yep." Besides, I really didn't want to be on my own today while Rogue tailed me. I looked back at Wilder to find him shaking his head at me. "That's sorted, Wilder. I'll call Scott and leave a message for him to get in touch with me instead of you. That frees you up to do whatever you need to do." I flashed him a smile, trying to win him over.

In the end, he muttered to himself and then said, "I'm not dumb, Harlow. I know you totally smoothed me over with that charm of yours. Next time I see you, I'm gonna need cake if we're gonna continue this type of relationship."

I frowned. "What type of relationship?"

A smile tugged at his lips. "This thing we've got going where I let you get away with shit that I shouldn't. And don't try and tell me I don't, 'cause I know I do."

"I'll totally bring you cake next time." I grinned at him. "And thank you for making me forget for a little bit just how sick I feel."

123

"Can we get a move on?" The woman interrupted our conversation, reminding me I had places to go.

"Where do you need me to take you?"

"Woolloongabba."

She seemed to be a woman who didn't waste words and that suited me fine today. The less speaking we did, the better.

Without a backwards glance at Wilder or Rogue, I headed to my car. Once inside, I sent a text to Scott to ask him to call me instead of Wilder and then I turned to the woman who had settled into the seat next to me. "I'm Harlow."

Untrusting brown eyes stared back at me. "Scarlett."

Again, very economical on the words. "Where in Woolloongabba do you need to go?"

She rattled off the address and then turned her head to stare out the window. As I drove, I stole glances at her and wondered what she had going on in her life to cause her so much anger.

"You always stare at people?" she asked without looking at me.

"Only people that intrigue me."

Her head whipped around and her gaze found mine in that moment before I had to look back out the windscreen. "There's nothing intriguing here, Harlow."

I shook my head in disagreement. "I meet a lot of people through my work and I think you're wrong. You've shown up twice now at the clubhouse and argued with men that most wouldn't dream of taking on. All for your brother. Not a lot of people would do that, and if that's not intriguing, I don't know what is." I coughed as I got the words out and grimaced through the pain while I swallowed. My hands tightened on the steering wheel, drawing Scarlett's attention.

"You got painkillers for that?" she asked.

"Yeah, I took some Advil this morning. It's probably about time for some more."

"I've got something better for you. After we pick up the t-shirts, I'll get it for you." Her words were direct and final, as if she expected no argument from me.

"T-shirts?" Maybe it was my fuzzy brain, but I couldn't figure out what she meant by that statement. Not to mention the way she assumed I wanted whatever she had to offer me for my sore throat.

"Yeah, the t-shirts I've gotta collect at Woolloongabba."

I frowned. "I thought I was dropping you off somewhere?"

She sighed as if I was exasperating her. "No, I've just gotta pick the shirts up and then take them home."

Glancing at her for a moment before turning back to watch where I was driving, I asked, "Where do you live?"

"In The Valley." She paused before asking, "Why is there a biker tailing you?"

My gaze flicked to the rear-view mirror and I sighed. "Because my boyfriend is trying to be kind to me while he's away. He asked that guy to keep on eye on me while I'm sick and make sure I'm okay."

"By the way you sighed, I'm taking that to mean you don't appreciate his kindness?"

"No, I do...I just don't like the guy he asked to help him. I'd prefer any of the other club members to this one."

She shifted in her seat and rested her feet against the dash as if we were old friends and she had every right in the world to do that. If we were in anyone else's car, I'd ask her to remove them, but I didn't care in my car, so I said nothing. "Why did you get involved with a biker in the first place?"

The way she asked this question made me think she thought hooking up with a biker was the worst decision in the world. And yet, there didn't seem to be any judgement in her tone. "Have you ever dated men who screwed you over?"

"Uh, yeah...haven't we all?"

I shook my head. "No, I don't think all women have, Scarlett. But I have, more than once. When I met Scott, I felt this instant awareness that he was as straight up as they came. And I was right – he's always been honest with me, treated me well and stayed loyal. I fell in love with a man, not a biker."

She silently processed that. "Why is there a sad tone in your voice?"

My brows pulled together. "What do you mean?"

"Just then, when you talked about him being loyal and treating you well, you sounded almost sad."

I gripped the steering wheel a little harder and ignored the tightening in my chest. Tears threatened at the back of my eyes and I furiously blinked them away. How had she picked up on that?

As I tried to figure out how to answer her, she pointed to the street coming up on the left. "Turn here."

I quickly indicated and made the turn, almost hitting a car because my focus had been diverted from driving to thinking about my guilt over taking Scott for granted after my miscarriage.

Scarlett straightened in her seat and said, "Jesus, are you trying to kill us today?"

Anger at myself took over, but I directed it at her. "Don't ask me anymore personal questions and we might make it there in one piece," I snapped while scowling at her.

She raised her brows and murmured, "I see I hit on a touchy subject."

"Yes. And not one I want to discuss."

We drove the rest of the way in silence, but I stewed on her question the whole way. By the time we arrived at our destination, I was tense with irritation and sick with my cold. Not a great combination.

And definitely not a mood to be in to deal with Rogue.

127

I waited outside the rundown old Queenslander Scarlett directed me to. The heat of the day and the lack of air conditioning in my car caused me to wait on the footpath. And this gave Rogue ample opportunity to harass me some more.

He lit a cigarette and sauntered my way, his eyes trailing down my body.

Asshole.

"I've known Scott Cole a long time and never once seen him this hung up on a chick. Gotta say, though, I'm hedging my bets as to how long this will last. My best guess is it won't take him long to get tired of you and he'll move on to new tits and ass soon."

I stared at him in disgust, knowing full well all he wanted was for me to take his bait and argue with him. It took all my willpower to remain silent, but I did. That only managed to make him try harder to elicit a response out of me.

Taking a step closer to me, he sneered, "You know I'm right so you've got no comeback, have you?"

Rogue was a good-looking man, but ugly was all I saw, and I wondered how many women had fallen for him and lived to regret it. I imagined that number to be high.

I took a step away from him, but his hand curled around my arm and held me in place. "Where do you think you're going? I'm talking to you," he barked, his dislike of me clear in his tone.

Holding his gaze, I pried his fingers from my arm and shoved him away. Not an easy thing to do because he packed some muscle on his body and I wasn't at my strongest while being sick. But I'd be damned if I didn't at least try. "Scott asked you to watch me, not talk to me, so I suggest you back off and leave me alone."

He stumbled backwards as I struggled to catch my breath. Anger sat heavy in my chest as my mind worked fast to figure out his next move. I was quickly learning that Rogue was the kind of man you had to be two steps ahead of at all times.

Darkness glinted in his eyes and his shoulders tensed as he steadied himself. "You fuckin' bitch," he spat and began moving closer again, however at that moment, Scarlett joined us and halted his progress.

"I don't know much about bikers, dude, but I'm guessing it's not a smart move to call another biker's woman a fucking bitch." She stared at Rogue, challenging him to argue with her. I had to give her credit – the woman had balls.

He turned his scowl her way. "Why don't you shut the fuck up and stay out of business that doesn't concern you?"

Before I could intercept – because, I really did think it was time to end this conversation with Rogue – she advanced on him. "Aren't you the big man, asshole? I bet if Harlow's man were here, you wouldn't even dream of saying this shit to her. Does it make your dick feel bigger by picking on a woman?"

Rogue's eyes bulged and the vein in his neck strained against his skin while his fists clenched.

Oh, shit.

I actually feared for Scarlett's life in that moment.

And then my phone rang, and I was almost certain it saved us both.

"Hi, baby," I answered the phone after checking caller ID and seeing it was Scott.

"What's wrong?" he demanded, and I could hear the alarm in his voice. "You sound off."

I swallowed back my fear as my heart pounded in my chest. Meeting Rogue's enraged glare, I replied, "I'm with Rogue and we're okay." I tried to put his mind at ease while also reminding Rogue that Scott knew who I was with today, and that if anything happened to me, Scott would be chasing him down first.

Rogue threw me one last filthy glare before turning and stalking back to his bike.

Thank you, God.

"Why do you sound so strange?" Scott asked. Although he was still questioning me, I could hear less concern in his voice than before.

"I'm with that woman who came to the clubhouse the other day. It's probably just that." This didn't even sound plausible to me; I doubted Scott would buy it, but my mind couldn't come up with anything else fast enough.

He was silent for a beat and then asked, "Is she giving you grief?"

"No, I'm actually driving her somewhere."

"Jesus, Harlow, why?"

"It's a long story and I'll tell you when you get home if you still want to know, but for now, she needs that cash back she gave you the other day."

"Griff will give it to you, but can you put her on the phone, I've got something to say to her," he said. Frustration laced his words and my worry for him grew.

He's got too much to deal with at the moment.

I did as he asked and passed the phone to Scarlett. "Scott wants to talk to you," I said as I handed it over.

She took it with a raise of her brows.

I tuned their conversation out and turned my attention to Rogue who sat on his bike watching us. My gut told me to be very wary of this man and I decided to ask Blade to check him out.

Scarlett ended the call with Scott and handed me back my phone. "He said he's going to get that Griff dude to get the money to me today. Thanks for organising that."

"No worries." I eyed the bags she held, which I presumed had her t-shirts in them. "Where do you need me to take you now? Just to your house?"

"Yeah, your guy said he'd get Griff to bring the money there, so that would be good." She eyed Rogue. "I see why you don't like that asshole. I'd be doing everything in my power to get rid of him if I were you."

I nodded. "I'm working on it."

Scott will be home soon and then everything will be all right.

★★★

"What are the t-shirts for?" I asked Scarlett as I watched her unpack them in her kitchen half an hour later.

"I sell them at the Southbank market on the weekends." She began stacking them in styles on her kitchen counter.

"Oh, okay." I had a friend who used to try to sell her art at those markets and never had any success, so I wondered if she was able to make much money doing that.

Her head snapped up and she shot me a dirty look. "Don't stand there and judge me for my job choice."

Whoa.

"I'm not judging you. The only thought running through my mind at the moment is whether you can pay your bills by doing that because I had a friend who was never able to when she sold her art there."

"I do well out of it, and the best thing is, I work for myself. I report to no one and I'm off the grid." I got the distinct impression she'd had this conversation many times. Her tone was almost defensive.

I opened my mouth to reply, but a cough took hold and I doubled over as it turned into a coughing fit. Pain

132

racked my body and I squeezed my eyes shut. This cold was the worst one I'd had in a long time.

Scarlett moved so she could place her hand on my back and rubbed it for me. When I finally stopped coughing, I straightened, and she said, "Grab a stool and sit for a moment while I make you some tea." She left me no room to argue and waited until I'd done as she said before exiting the room onto her balcony.

I folded my arms on the counter and rested my head on them while she was gone. My energy levels were rapidly deteriorating and I wasn't convinced I'd make it through a shift at the café today.

A couple of minutes later, the door behind me slid open and I lifted my head to see Scarlett circling the kitchen bench. She busied herself with boiling the kettle and crushing some leaves that looked to be Thyme leaves.

Her home was a tiny, old apartment that had an even tinier balcony off the kitchen, and from what I'd glimpsed, plants filled that area. The small kitchen barely fit both of us and was in dire need of renovation. Tiles were beginning to peel off the wall and the discoloured and worn countertop looked like it was out of the seventies.

As she reached into the cupboard for a mug, she said, "Thyme tea will help your cough, but I think you need a lot of rest because you seem pretty run down."

"I can't rest, I have too much to do at the moment."

"Sometimes your body gives you no choice." She placed the leaves in the mug and poured hot water over them. Turning to face me, she said, "What's so important that it means you can't take some time for you?"

I rested my elbows on the counter and then placed my face in my hands. "I'm working two jobs plus looking out for my sick neighbours."

She shrugged. "So call in sick."

"I can't. One of the jobs is at my Mum's café and the other job is at one of Storm's clubs. They need all the help they can get, so I can't let them down." As the words fell out of my mouth, I began crying.

Geez.

Wiping at the tears, I apologised, "Sorry about this. I have no idea why I'm crying." Embarrassment at breaking down in front of a stranger filled me, but the more I tried to hide my tears, the more they came.

Scarlett didn't move to console me. She simply remained where she stood across the island bench from me, and said, "You must have needed to get them out. Maybe you should talk about it."

"I don't even know you."

"Sometimes it's good to talk to a complete stranger about shit. I find they don't have the preconceived thoughts and feelings about you that your friends and family do."

She's right.

"Oh, God." I took a deep breath through my tears and then let my thoughts tumble out of my mouth. "I feel like I'm only just holding everything together at the moment, including myself. And it feels like if one thing gave way, everything else would crumble with it. But I need to keep it together for Scott..." My voice trailed off as I reached for the tissue she was holding out to me.

"What's this bullshit about holding it together for Scott? He's your boyfriend, right?"

"Yes."

"So why does he expect you to hold it all together for him?"

"No, he doesn't...I'm not explaining this very well...Scott's got a lot on with his club at the moment and I don't want to burden him any more than I already have." Between my sore throat and foggy mind, I was finding it difficult to explain myself.

Scarlett bent at the waist and leant her forearms on the counter. Her voice softened from the hardness it had previously held, and her eyes glossed over with a new softness as she said, "You know, sometimes we tell ourselves that our loved ones expect us to say and do things a certain way or that they expect stuff from us that they really don't. From the little you've told me about Scott, I bet he's the kind of guy who would prefer you focus on getting yourself better rather than running yourself ragged, trying to do all these things."

I stared at her for a long moment before baring my soul. "We lost a baby a little while ago and I've really let him down. I don't want to let him down any more," I whispered.

Her forehead crinkled in a frown. "How do you figure you let him down by losing a baby? It's not like you chose to lose the baby."

Shaking my head, I rushed to explain. "No, I didn't let him down by losing the baby, but I shut him out. He gave me all the support I needed and I pushed him away. And on top of that, I wasn't there for him." I paused as memories of what Scott and I had been through flooded my mind. *I really did let him down.* "He lost a baby, too, and I wasn't there for *him*." My voice cracked and a sob escaped.

As more tears fell, she remained silent, and I appreciated her lack of rushing to console me. It was what everyone I knew did whenever tears threatened – they tried to hug me and tell me everything would be okay. I wanted to scream at them that as much as a hug and a few words of encouragement were appreciated, they would never fix the hole in my heart. Sometimes, the only thing you could do was live through the pain – let it take its grip, let it almost kill you, and then when you thought you couldn't take another step forward, you had to find the courage to do just that. Sometimes, you had to let the pain heal you in the only way it could – by showing you how much strength you had buried deep. Pain could wound like a motherfucker, but it could also teach you what you were made of.

And yet, as much as my pain had taught me, I still struggled to let go of my guilt.

Scarlett finally spoke when my tears began to subside. "When we fuck up in life, we can't go back and have a do-over. But what we can do is decide *never* to do that shit again, and then do everything in our power to do it right from then on. And, Harlow? That's a shitload of guilt you're carrying around with you, and I bet it's not only hurting you, but also your relationship with Scott. You need to get the fuck over that guilt, reposition your lady-balls and move the fuck on. Stop wallowing in that because it's making you be less than what you are."

Well, shit...

I raised my brows at her. "Do you always give such blunt and honest advice?"

"Yes. What's the point in giving advice that's not honest?" Her eyes didn't leave mine; it was like she was challenging me to argue with her, but I couldn't fault her logic.

"True." I knew she was right, but putting her advice into action was a whole other story, especially when I had another thing on my mind. "My period is late," I finally admitted the one thing I hadn't told anyone yet; the one thing I wasn't sure to be happy or concerned about.

She reached for the mug of tea she'd slid in front of me a moment ago and tipped its contents down the sink before asking, "How late?"

I frowned. "Why did you throw that away?"

"You can't drink that if you're pregnant; I don't know if it would harm the baby or not. How late are you?"

"A week. My period has always been on time; even after my miscarriage it got back on track straight away."

She sighed like she was frustrated with me. "So you either need to go to the doctor or take a test." Even her voice held a frustrated tone.

I sat up straight and glared at her. "Why are you sighing at me like that?"

"Because women annoy the shit out of me sometimes. You all make shit harder than it has to be. If your period is late when it's never late, do the math and figure that shit out. Don't just spend a week worrying over it – that doesn't help you at all."

Crossing my arms over my chest, I said, "Did it ever occur to you that some women might need that extra time to get used to the idea?"

"Did it ever occur to you that that's a bullshit excuse for not dealing with your problems?"

Annoyance moved me off the stool. Swiping my keys off her kitchen counter, I snapped, "No, it's not. Women are emotional creatures, and I, for one, need time to process my emotions over stuff."

As I walked down her hallway to the front door, she followed me. "I know all about emotions, Harlow, and what I've learnt through all the shit in my life is that they don't necessarily serve you very well. Look at the facts instead – they never let you down."

I didn't want to spend any more time listening to her advice or getting into an argument with her so I ignored that and kept going. When I opened the front door, I came face-to-face with Griff.

"Harlow?" He seemed confused about my presence.

"Don't even ask, Griff," I muttered, and moved past him. I didn't stop to look back, but rather headed straight to my car. The sooner I got to the café and my mum, the sooner I'd feel better. Between my cold, my worry over Scott and the club, Rogue tailing me, and thoughts of being pregnant again, this day was one I wanted over and done with as fast as possible.

Chapter Nine
Scott

Three Days Later

"Julio is bad news, brother. If I were you, I'd be helping him take his last breath."

I rubbed the back of my neck as I listened to King tell me what I already knew. Nash, J and I had just arrived back at the clubhouse after our trip home from Adelaide. King had left a message on my phone so I'd called him straight back in case he had some new information for us. All I really wanted to do was get to Harlow – six days without her and I was edgy as hell. "I just got back from Adelaide. Bourne wants us to help him get rid of Julio so he can take over his territory."

"Why does he need your help?"

"Good question. Says he needs his hands clean to avoid retaliation from Julio's allies, but I can't help think there's more to this I'm not seeing." My stomach grumbled with hunger and exhaustion washed over me as my mind continued to search for the answer that felt just out of reach.

King remained silent for a few moments and I imagined his mind also looking for an answer. "Bourne's a sneaky bastard, for sure, but I can't see how helping him on this could hurt you. From what I've learnt of Julio, he'll work to gather allies in Queensland and eventually *that* could hurt you, so getting rid of him can only be a good thing. And to have Bourne owe you can never be a bad thing."

This was the same conclusion I'd come to. "Thanks for looking into it," I said before we ended the call.

"King had nothing new?" J asked.

"No."

"Fuck," J muttered. The three of us were in agreement over our distrust of Bourne and what his true agenda was, and we'd been hoping King would be able to shed some light on it for us.

"Yeah, fuck is about right," I agreed as we headed inside.

Inside to Harlow.

Club members filled the clubhouse. Four o'clock in the afternoon signalled it was time to wind down for the day - time for a drink with your brothers before heading home to your old lady.

I pushed my way through the crowd, doing my best not to get side-tracked from my end goal, but fifteen minutes later and I was still stuck talking to some of the guys who were anxious to know how our trip had panned out.

Fuck.

My dick was getting as frustrated as the rest of me.

And then a loud whistle sounded and the voice that caused my dick to go from frustrated to hard in less than a second, sounded. "Boys, you've had your turn with my man. Now it's my time."

Wolf whistles and dirty cheers erupted as my eyes finally landed on the woman I'd missed like fuck.

She came to me with a sexy smile and reached straight for my ass with both hands. "Next time you go away, consider taking me with you," she said before kissing me.

No fucking arguments there.

Fuck, her lips and body were teasing me with promises of the kind of sex that six days away from your woman would lead to.

I ended the kiss and moved my mouth close to her ear. "Baby, I'm not letting you out of my sight ever again. And I hope like fuck that you're ready for a long night."

She moaned as I ground myself against her. "It's a good thing I'm feeling better now."

Thank God she was feeling better. I'd been concerned about her, but Mum had finally reported yesterday that she was doing much better. And who would have thought me going away would lead Harlow and my mother to bond in the way they had. Just another thing to add to my list of '*Shit I'll Never Understand, But Am Thankful For*'.

I ran my hand over her ass and up her back. When I found her hair, I took hold and pulled her head back so I could dip my mouth to her neck. *Fuck, she smells good.* I kissed her and as she moaned again, I added my teeth to the kiss, and fuck if she didn't arch her back and press her front to me harder.

Pulling away, I rasped, "Jesus, woman, I need to get you out of here, otherwise your ass is gonna be planted on that couch and my dick is gonna be buried so far deep in you before you can stop me."

Her mouth turned up in a grin, but she didn't say anything.

"What?" I demanded.

"There is no way Scott Cole is going to fuck his woman in front of his club, but I love your enthusiasm. Personally, I think these guys are so involved in their drinking that we could probably have sex on that couch and none of them would even notice."

143

I raised my brows. "You wanna see just where Scott Cole would fuck his woman? 'Cause I'm happy to show you."

Her grin grew. "I dare you, baby."

Fuck.

She knows me too fucking well and she's fucking playing me.

I kept my gaze trained on her while I pulled out my phone and called Griff. When he answered, I said, "You guys right if I head home for the night?"

"Yeah, brother. We've got it under control. Church is scheduled for ten in the morning and then we've got the re-opening of Trilogy tomorrow night."

My gaze dropped to Harlow's lips as she licked them, and my dick begged for that tongue. I raised my finger to her lips and closed her mouth, holding my finger there as I replied, "See you in the morning."

Shoving my phone in my pocket, I growled, "I want you outside. *Now.*"

Her grin disappeared and gave way to a sexy curl of her lips. Without another word, she turned and began walking outside. My eyes dropped to her ass. The way it swayed under the tight fit of her short, black dress almost made me come in my pants.

That dress is fucking perfect.

I followed her outside and as we walked past the corner of the building, I snagged her around the waist, lifted her to rest against my body and carried her around

144

the corner. I then deposited her on the ground and pushed her up against the building. My hands went to the hem of her dress and I pulled it up to reveal her panties. I slid one hand inside to find her pussy while my other hand moved to take hold of her chin.

My eyes found hers and I demanded, "You good if I fuck my woman now?"

Those beautiful eyes of hers widened and she nodded. Her arms came around my neck, and she said, "I thought you were going to make me wait until we got home."

My heart sped up and my self-control almost reached breaking point. "Harlow, six days without your pussy and I'm ready to snap my dick off and suck it myself, but even that wouldn't be enough. I need *you.* I'm not sure you realise how fuckin' whipped for you I am. No way in hell can I wait until we get home."

She wrapped one leg around me and used it to lift herself off the ground and into my arms while wrapping her other leg around me at the same time. Then her lips came to mine and she kissed me with the same desperate need I had for her. Her lips were almost brutal and her tongue demanded nothing less than everything I had to give, until the point we were both panting.

When the kiss ended, we stared at each other through wild eyes for a moment.

She's mine, but I need more.

I need her like I've never needed anyone.

I need forever.

145

"What?" she panted out as we clung to each other in that suspended-in-time moment.

"I need you, Harlow."

"You have me, baby."

"No, I need more. I want forever with you." My mind raced with the words I couldn't quite find to make her understand, and my chest pumped harder as my urgency grew.

"We have forever, Scott. I want that, too." Her words came out fast, like she was trying to hurry me, but as much as I needed to be inside her, I needed to make her grasp what I was asking for.

"Marry me." Fuck, I'd never imagined proposing to Harlow when I had her pushed up against a wall with her dress around her waist and my dick bulging out of my pants, but life hardly ever went the way I envisioned.

Understanding finally dawned in her eyes, and her face lit up with a huge smile. "That's a given, but you're going to have to give me a proper proposal before I actually say yes."

Her sass was one of the reasons I loved her and she didn't let me down. I shook my head and muttered, "Of course I fuckin' am. But let's be clear – we *are* getting married and it *will* be soon."

She tightened her arms around me. "The only thing we need to be clear about right this minute is the fact you're going to get your dick out real soon and fuck me. Turns out I'm a cranky bitch when my man goes away, so you need to fix that fast. And I bet when I'm no longer cranky, you can get me to agree to all sorts of things."

"Fuck," I growled. "I'm having second thoughts about taking you away with me next time. Turns out I fuckin' love your dirty mouth when you're a cranky bitch."

She opened her mouth but before she could get any words out, I crashed my mouth down onto hers and stole her breath with a kiss. The way she groaned into it and pushed her body against mine told me she loved it.

While I kissed her, I reached down and undid my pants to free my cock. I slid Harlow's panties to the side and positioned her so I could enter her.

Finally.

Fuck.

She was so damn wet and ready for me, welcoming me home. Her pussy squeezed around my dick and my eyes closed as I enjoyed the fuck out of that.

And then I pulled out and thrust back in.

And I knew I'd never go six days without her again.

As I held her tight and fucked her hard, I managed to get out, "This is going to be fast, baby."

She gripped me hard and fought for her release as hard as I did. And as we worked together to find the magic we always found, I knew I'd always fight hard for her.

For absolutely every part of her.

The sex.

The good times.

147

The bad times.

And the sweet, sweet moments where I knew no matter how much shit we had to go through, we'd make it.

Chapter Ten
Harlow

"Six days away from J, and I was going crazy," Madison said as we watched Scott and J on the other side of the restaurant.

It was the night after they'd returned from their trip, and we were at the re-opening of Storm's restaurant, Trilogy. Most of the club members were in attendance, along with their old ladies.

I turned to Madison with a frown. "Griff's not here. He's coming, right?"

"As far as I know, he is. But can we get back to more important things, please?"

"What?" I was so distracted tonight. Scott had asked me to marry him last night, and yet, I still hadn't told him I was pregnant.

Nerves whooshed through me at the thought.

I'm pregnant.

I'd left Scarlett's house in a shitty mood the other day, but after spending hours contemplating everything she'd said, I realised she was right. As much as that pained me to admit. And so I'd taken a test, and it confirmed my pregnancy. I'd then proceeded to call in sick to all my jobs and ignored my phone except to take calls from Scott, my mother, Sharon and Cassie.

The last three days had been spent doing some deep soul searching while resting and making art, and I'd come to the decision I was okay with being pregnant. Actually, I was more than okay with it – I was ecstatic. But I was also scared of losing the baby, and perhaps that was why I hadn't told anyone yet. I knew it was crazy, but telling people made it real. And real meant I had to face my fears because I was sure once Scott knew, he'd want to talk out all my concerns.

"Harlow! Are you even paying attention?" Madison demanded.

I blinked. "I'm sorry. Tell me what's going on in your world." I reached for the water in front of me and took a long sip.

"J came home last night and I was ready to jump his bones, and while he did have sex with me, I could tell he really just wanted to go to sleep."

"And?"

"Do you think that means there's something going on that he's not telling me about? Remember the last time he shut down on me was because of a secret he was keeping."

Scarlett's words came back to haunt me - *You all make shit harder than it has to be.*

She's right.

"Madison, if you think there's something wrong, just ask him. It's the only way you'll know for sure." My voice was a little snippy when I didn't mean for it to be.

She stared at me. "Are you okay?"

"Why? Do I not seem okay?"

"You seem off. Are you still feeling sick?"

Her voice held concern, but I didn't want to get into a conversation about it with her. She'd figure it out fast and I didn't want anyone to figure it out before I told Scott. Grappling for something to divert her attention, I was relieved when I saw Griff enter the restaurant...with a woman.

"Holy shit," I murmured. "Who is that with Griff?" Whoever she was, she was stunning. And he held her close, in the way a man held a woman he loved.

Madison followed my gaze and almost choked on her drink. "Geez, Griff's been holding out."

151

We both watched in amazement as Griff led the beautiful blonde our way. His eyes held a warning, and I knew not to make a big scene about this new development in his life. Griff was a very private man and if he kept a woman to himself, I figured he had a good reason. And he was entitled to his privacy.

"Ladies," he greeted us, his arm firmly around his woman's waist. "I'd like you to meet my girlfriend, Sophia."

Madison practically jumped out of her chair in excitement. "It's so good to meet you!" she exclaimed. "I'm Madison and this is Harlow."

I expected Sophia to shrink from Madison and her overly excited greeting, but instead, a smile graced her face, and she easily stepped out of Griff's hold. "It's so lovely to meet you both."

Griff whispered something in her ear and she nodded. He then brushed a quick kiss across her lips and left us.

As we all watched him go, Madison murmured, "Griff always did know how to keep a secret."

Sophia took the seat next to Madison's and when she eyed the wine bottle in the middle of the table, asked, "Can I *please* have some of your wine? It's been a long day and to say I'm a little nervous about meeting everyone tonight is an understatement. Griff's been holding back on introducing me, wanting time just for us, and while I'm the kind of woman who is willing to wait for my man to get stuff sorted in his mind, I've been dying to meet you all. And then he just announced last night that tonight was the night, and I kinda went into panic mode. You know, the whole, 'what will I wear', and 'I've gotta get my hair done', and 'holy shit, I need new shoes'... So I'm thinking a glass or two of wine right about now would be good." She stopped rambling and took a deep breath while eyeing us with the kind of look a woman gives another woman when they desperately need to be understood.

I couldn't help it, I laughed. Pushing the wine bottle her way, I said, "Knock yourself out. And can I just say, you are not at all the kind of woman I ever expected Griff to date. And I mean that in the best possible way."

She poured herself a glass of wine, took a sip, and then said, "We're a little bit different, yes."

Madison had sat back down, and was staring at Sophia in what could only be described as wonder. Leaning her elbows on the table, she demanded, "Tell us everything – how you met Griff, how long you've been dating, all about you...we need to know *everything*."

Sophia drank some more wine before placing her glass on the table and telling us everything Madison wanted to know. We were still deep in conversation twenty minutes later when Velvet arrived, and I'd already decided I loved Sophia. She was the kind of woman I loved to hang out with – funny, kind and honest – and I could see exactly why Griff had chosen her.

As Velvet took a seat and Madison made introductions, I excused myself to go to the bathroom.

The atmosphere in the restaurant was electric. Storm had worked long hours to get Trilogy back up and running, and the guys were celebrating hard. I made my way to the bathroom fairly easily, but got held up on my way back, so decided to backtrack and find another way through to my table.

Lost in my thoughts, I ran into Griff. "Whoa, Harlow, you okay?" he asked after we collided.

"Sorry, I was miles away." I smiled up at him. "I love Sophia, and I'm really glad you finally introduced us."

Griff was a man of few words and even less facial expressions, and he didn't let me down. He simply nodded and said, "Figured it was time to bring her into the club."

The way he said it made me think he could be making their relationship permanent, but I didn't push him for more. The little he'd given me was probably all he planned on sharing.

"You do realise you've lost her to Madison now, right? At least for some hours every week. She's planning weekly get-togethers for the Storm women now."

His lips twitched and he nodded again. "Figured that would happen. Sophia will love that."

As I stood watching him and thinking about how much his life was changing, two hands slid around my waist and warm breath tickled my ear. "By my calculations there are about three more hours of tonight left before I can take

154

you home and practice my proposal to you again. Don't drink too much tonight, sweetheart, because I'm planning the longest fuckin' proposal known to man."

It should have been lust that whooshed through me at his words, but instead, guilt hit me fair in the chest.

I need to tell him there will be no more drinking for me for nine months.

I'll tell him tonight.

Later.

Before I could respond, Griff's phone rang and he gave Scott a perplexed look. Scott's body tensed against mine as we listened to Griff's call.

"Why are you calling me?" He spoke into the phone with irritation. "We settled the cash the other day which cleared up everything between you and the club."

Silence while he listened, and then – "That shit's between you, your brother and whoever the fuck he's buying drugs from."

He listened some more before moving his phone away from his mouth and saying to Scott, "It's that chick we gave that money back to the other day...Says she's got some drug dealers threatening her."

"What the fuck does she want us to do about it?" Scott asked as he ran one of his hands over my ass. His body against mine and his hands all over me turned me on, but guilt still filled my mind, as did concern for Scarlett.

"She wants us to go to her house and help her."

155

"Jesus, she kicks me in the balls and then wants my help?" Scott muttered.

Griff nodded and opened his mouth to say something, but I cut in. "I think we should help her. Scarlett doesn't strike me as the kind of person who asks for help unless she really needs it."

Scott let me go and moved next to me. "Well, she strikes me as the kind of woman who can take care of herself."

I raised my brows at him. "You're really gonna let a woman calling for help fend for herself?"

He raked his fingers through his hair. "Fuck..." Eyeing Griff, he said, "I'll take Wilder with me, check it out. You right to keep the party going here?"

"Yeah, you guys go." He put the phone back to his ear. "Scott will be there soon." When he hung up, he said to Scott, "I'll text you the address."

"I'll go with you and show you where she lives," I said.

Scott's eyes darted to mine and he shook his head. "Fuck, no. I don't want you anywhere near this."

"Surely I'll be safe if I'm with you."

"No," his voice was firm, "I want you to stay here. If I take you with me, I won't be able to concentrate on anything but you, and that will put everyone at risk."

The baby.

"You're right," I said softly as I reached for his hand. "Please be safe."

His face softened and he squeezed my hand. Dipping his face to mine, he kissed me. "I'm always safe, sweetheart," he tried to reassure me, but my gut swirled with apprehension. Maybe it was the thought of our child, but I had a bad feeling about something.

I reached my hand around his neck and pulled him back for another longer kiss. "I love you," I whispered, trying to keep the fear from my voice.

He frowned. "What's wrong?"

"Nothing." I placed my hands on his chest and pasted a smile on my face. "You should go in case Scarlett really needs you."

Keeping his attention focused on me for another few moments, he stayed silent, but I knew my man, and he was still trying to decide if I needed him. Eventually he said, "Okay, but if you need me, you call."

"I will," I promised and watched as he left.

Turning to Griff, I said, "Can you please let me know if something happens while they are with Scarlett."

His forehead creased. "You sound worried."

"I *am* worried, Griff. I'm not sure why, but I am. I never ask to be involved in club business and I'm not now, but I would like to be kept in the loop on Scott. Please." The unease hadn't left me, so I held my ground with Griff. I would not finish this conversation until he gave me his word he would do what I asked.

157

He contemplated my request and I thought for sure he'd argue with me, but he didn't. "I'll let you know how it goes."

"Thank you."

I left him and headed back to the girls.

God, I hope my gut is wrong.

I want to marry that man.

Chapter Eleven
Scott

The last thing I wanted to be doing was checking in on a woman who'd been nothing but a pain in my ass since we'd first met. It's funny what the woman you love can convince you to do. However, as I stood in Scarlett's tiny kitchen and listened to what she had to say, I sensed there was something to her concerns.

"Tell me exactly what he said," I demanded. She'd just described a run-in she had that day with a guy in a supermarket car park, and he sounded like he had ties to Julio.

"He threatened to disable my brother if he didn't pay up within two days, and then he said he knew I was connected to Storm and that I should tell you guys to watch your backs."

I frowned. "I thought you'd paid your brother's debt?"

Her shoulders tensed. "I did. This is a new debt."

"Fuck," Wilder muttered. "Why are you paying his debts?"

"Because he's dead if I don't," she stated, as if the answer was obvious.

"Have you got the cash?" I asked.

She swallowed hard and met my gaze. "No. I've got some, but not all of it."

"Okay, let's back this up. Did he say anything else? We need something more so we can figure out who he is," I said, my mind racing as I tried to piece this together. It had to be someone either watching her or watching us, and my bet was on someone watching *us*.

She rubbed the back of her neck and I caught sight of Wilder's attention being diverted to her chest. I didn't give a shit what he did with his time, but I needed his attention completely on Storm at the moment, so I shook my head at him when I caught his gaze. He nodded and quickly glanced back at her face.

"He didn't say anything else to me, but I did overhear him on the phone as he walked away from me...something about a Julio," she finally said, giving us the name we needed.

I pulled my phone out to call Griff, however the sound of glass smashing diverted my attention. Wilder reached for his gun at the same time I reached for mine.

Signalling to him, I said, "Front window?"

"Sounds like it, brother."

"Stay here while we investigate," I said to Scarlett and after she'd nodded her agreement, we headed to the front of her apartment.

Scarlett's apartment was old and shabby, as were the sheer curtains on her front windows. Along with the outside light she had left on, they made it easy to see the two guys standing on the front balcony. A gush of wind caused the curtain to blow to the side just as one of the guys spotted us and raised his gun to take aim.

"Fuck!" I yelled, at the same time as Wilder shoved me to the ground.

The gun sounded and thankfully the bullet missed us. I scrambled to my feet and closed the distance to the front door. Yanking it open, I ducked to avoid the fist coming my way. And then another gun sounded, confusing the hell out of me because it wasn't either of these two guys, and it sounded like it came from behind us.

"Get the fuck out of my apartment!" Scarlett yelled, and tension punched through me at the thought of her getting caught up in this.

"Jesus, Scott, she's got a fucking gun!" Wilder roared.

He wasn't telling me anything I didn't know, and while I wanted to go to her and rip that gun from her hands and

161

tell her to get the fuck back, I was dealing with more pressing matters – one guy trying to knock me out and another waving a gun around.

As I straightened, I punched the guy in his stomach.

"Motherfucker," he yelled, stumbling backwards.

Aiming my gun at both of them, I thundered, "Who the fuck are you?" I didn't recognise either of them, cementing my belief they were from Julio's crew, but I needed confirmation.

"It doesn't matter *who* we are, all that matters is *why* we're here," the guy with the gun snarled as he raised it at me.

"*Why* you're here is pretty fuckin' clear," I snapped. My brain worked overtime trying to figure out how the fuck this was going to go down.

He smirked. "Nothing's ever as it seems."

What the hell?

My finger twitched on the trigger of the gun, but I refrained from pulling it. I needed to confirm who they were. However, before I could do that, Scarlett pulled the trigger on her gun, and all hell broke loose.

She shot at the roof, but it spooked the two guys and the one with the gun also fired his. Thank fuck my reflexes were quick – I ducked in time to avoid being shot.

"Fuck, Wilder, can you restrain her?" I yelled.

"I'm already on it," he threw back and I blocked out their arguing as I did my best to defend all three of us.

162

I lifted my leg and kicked the guy in front of me as hard as I could in the stomach, which pushed him backwards into the one with the gun. He dropped the gun, so before either had a chance to recover, I moved to kick it out of reach. They were scrambling to get to their feet, and the panic I read on their faces put my mind at ease. It looked like I was about to get to the bottom of who sent them.

Standing over them, I aimed my gun again, and demanded, "Tell me who the fuck you work for or - " I directed my gun at one of the guy's dicks, " – shit's about to get real fuckin' messy."

Fear sliced across his face and he held his hands up. "Stop! It's Julio...he sent us."

"Why?" I asked, keeping my gun aimed at his dick.

He opened his mouth to speak, but his mate silenced him by slitting his throat from behind with a knife I'd never seen coming. As the guy slumped back with blood oozing from his throat, his mate shoved his body to the side so he could stand. Everything happened so fast – one minute I had the situation under control, and the next the tables had been turned.

I did the only thing I could in that moment – I shot him.

As his breath was stolen from him, so was our chance at gaining new information about Julio.

I raked my fingers through my hair and turned to face Wilder. He held Scarlett around her waist, but now that the threat had been erased, he let her go.

"You good?" I asked her.

"Yeah, but damn that's a mess," she said, nodding at the dead men and blood on the floor of her apartment.

Wilder stepped over the bodies and closed the front door. Eyeing me, he said, "We need to get this shit cleaned up before any cops turn up."

I called Griff. "We need some help here, brother," I said when he answered.

After I filled him in on what had happened, and he told me J and Nash were on their way, he said, "This complicates shit."

"Yeah."

"We need to start calling in favours, Scott. Once Julio figures this out, we're gonna need our backs covered."

Fuck.

Not the way I wanted shit to go down.

Chapter Twelve
Scott

I stood at the end of our bed and watched as Harlow slid her dress over her head. Something was different about her, but I hadn't been able to put my finger on it. After I'd dealt with the mess at Scarlett's home last night, I'd headed straight back to Trilogy and she'd been beside herself with worry. I'd never seen her so consumed with fear before, but I hadn't been able to convince her to share those fears with me.

As she smoothed her dress, she looked over at me. "How long do you think Scarlett will have to stay here with us?"

I'd made the decision to bring Scarlett with us when we left her apartment last night. No way was she safe in her own place. Not until we dealt with Julio. "Hopefully not long." I hadn't shared with her the events of last night except to let her know Scarlett wasn't safe.

She watched me for another couple of moments before finally nodding and saying, "Okay."

I moved to where she stood and wrapped my hand around her wrist, halting her as she took a step away from me. "Are you pissed off with me for bringing her here?" I couldn't read her and it frustrated me.

"No." She tried to pull her wrist free, but I gripped it tighter.

Christ.

Why won't she talk to me?

Pulling her close, I ran my free hand through her hair. "Harlow, what's going on? You've been off ever since I got back from Scarlett's last night."

She sighed. "It will sound stupid."

"Try me."

After a moment of hesitation, she finally opened up. "I have this weird feeling deep in my gut that something bad is going to happen to you. Last night I was really worried and then you came back with Scarlett and said she wasn't safe, and I'm still feeling sick with worry. You never exaggerate things, so for you to bring her here tells me you're worried, too."

I let her wrist go. "It's true, I *am* worried. But we have this covered, so I want you to go to work and try not to think about it too much, okay?"

Her eyes searched mine and then she said, "I will."

"Can you take Scarlett with you? I don't have enough men to spare one to stay with her today."

"I'm happy for her to come to the café with me, but good luck convincing her to do anything."

She had a point – convincing Scarlett to leave her apartment last night had been a tough gig. "I've got an idea of how to talk her into it. Let's see if she goes for it."

Loud banging on the front door interrupted our conversation, and I left her to see who it was.

"Mr Cole, we finally meet." Two cops stood on the other side of the door. I knew they were detectives because I'd come across one of them before.

I planted my legs wide and crossed my arms over my chest. "What can I do for you?"

The short, pudgy one at the front that I'd never met before took a step to enter the house, but I put my arm out to block him. He raised his brows. "We've got things to discuss."

I didn't budge. "Those things can be discussed here."

A scowl flashed across his face. "Some new evidence has come to light with regards to your father's death."

167

"What kind of evidence?" They'd come up with nothing solid so far, and I suspected they were simply on a fishing expedition.

His chin jutted as smugness glinted in his eyes. "Evidence that points to your club."

Bullshit.

We'd made sure there was no evidence.

I crossed my arms again, not backing down. "So you're going to interview me?"

A brief flicker of hesitation passed over his face and he stalled for a second. Not the body language of a confident man. He tried to cover it, but I didn't miss it. "Not a formal interview yet, but we would like to talk to you about it and - "

I cut him off. "Either you call me in for an interview or we don't talk. I'm not talking to you off the record."

The tall detective at the back who was familiar to me, but who I was having trouble placing, took over. "We'll be in touch." Even his voice was familiar, but my memory was a tangled mess and I couldn't place him. He tapped the short one on the shoulder to indicate they were leaving, and in that moment, I realised he held the power in that relationship.

I called Griff as I watched them leave. "You had any cops sniffing around about Marcus's death?"

"No. Have you?"

"Yeah. Harlow told me they called around while I was away, and they've just shown up again, saying they have

168

new evidence that points to the club. When I called their bluff, they caved. They also sussed Mum out, but she didn't give them anything. I'm just trying to figure out what their game is because we covered our tracks thoroughly."

He was quiet for a moment and then said, "I'll do some digging, see what I can find out."

We ended the call and I headed back into the house to find Harlow. I ran into Scarlett on the way, and took a moment to talk to her about spending the day at the café.

"I need you to hang out with Harlow today so I can be sure of your safety. You good with that?"

She frowned. "Not really what I had planned for the day."

The woman is a pain in my ass.

"What do you have planned?"

"I need to find my brother and make sure he's okay."

"So how about you let me do that while you go with Harlow?"

Her eyes narrowed at me. "Really?"

I raked my fingers through my hair. It was going to be a long, fucking day. "Yes, really."

She rested her weight on one foot and cocked her head. "Why would you do that for me?"

"Jesus, Scarlett, are you this untrusting with everyone?"

"Yes."

169

"Well you're gonna have to ease up a little with me and start putting some faith in what I say. We're all in this shit together now. I can keep you safe, but that's gonna involve you doing what I say. And no more fuckin' guns when I'm in the middle of handling a situation."

We watched each other while she worked that through in her mind. Eventually, she said, "Okay, but can you do me a favour?"

"Fuck, as if I'm not already doing you one?" The woman was something else.

She threw me a glare. "Can you lend me some money so I can pay off his debt?"

I blew out a long breath. "Scarlett, I'm going to sort shit so that your brother has no fuckin' debt to pay off, and then I'm going to sort more shit so that he never gets a fuckin' debt again." I raised my brows at her. "You good with that?"

"You're a moody biker, aren't you?"

Harlow had joined us and snorted.

I ignored her.

"Give me your brother's address," I said as I pulled out my phone to store it in.

"You know, manners never went out of fashion," she muttered.

Harlow's snort turned into a laugh and as she walked past us, she threw over her shoulder, "I think having you here is going to be fun, Scarlett."

Scarlett and I glared at Harlow's back before she finally gave me her brother's address.

I typed it into my phone and then shot back at whoever the fuck was listening, "*I'm* not seeing any fuckin' joy in this situation."

Women.

"Motherfucker!" I roared as we received yet another rejection. We'd spent the last four hours trying to call in favours around town and most had said they couldn't chance giving Storm their support against Julio who had already found a way to blackmail them into taking his back.

Griff rubbed the back of his neck. "We're running out of options here, brother. And when I do finally get the chance, I'm gonna take great fucking delight in making Julio feel pain for this."

My phone rang and as I answered it, I said to Griff, "It's Colt, hopefully he has some good news for us." He'd also been trying to find support for Storm.

"Got some bad news for you, Scott," he said. "Most of the guys I've spoken to today say their hands are tied, so at this point I've only been able to convince two crews to take our back."

"We've had the same," I told him. "You done with your list yet?"

"I've got one more to visit and then I'm heading back to the clubhouse."

"Thanks, man."

I hung up and eyed Griff. "He's got two so far."

"It's fucked, but at least it's better than none. Have you spoken to Blade yet?"

I shook my head. "No, but I will be."

My phone sounded with a text.

Harlow: I know you're busy but wanted to let you know that Lisa and Michelle are doing much better today. I checked in on them after you left this morning.

Me: Thanks, baby. You girls okay?

Harlow: Yes, but I'm disappointed.

Me: Why?

Harlow: You didn't practice your proposal last night.

Me: It's on my list for tonight.

Harlow: Good. Just wanted to make you smile. Hope your day isn't too shitty.

Me: Trust me, you made me smile. See you tonight.

As I sent my last text to Harlow, Bourne called me.

"What's up, Bourne?" I asked, keen to get this phone call over with fast.

"I'm wondering where you and I stand? I never did hear back from you after you left Adelaide."

"I'm putting together a plan to deal with Julio."

"Good. The sooner the better."

"Let's get one thing straight here, Bourne – once this is done, you'll owe me, and when I come calling on that favour, you won't hesitate to say yes." No need for him to know I was already working on this plan before he asked me to do it.

Silence for a moment, and then – "Agreed."

"I'll let you know when it's done." I hung up without waiting for his response.

"Just for the record, again, I truly despise that asshole," Griff said.

I let the tension in my body go and blew out a harsh breath. "I'm with you on that."

After we left the last place we visited, we walked the block back to where we left our bikes. Reaching for his helmet, Griff said, "You wanna try Scarlett's brother again?"

We had visited his place this morning and he wasn't home. I nodded. "Yeah, let's see if we have better luck this time. And then we need to check in with J and Nash to see if they have anything new on Julio."

Surely we've gotta have some luck somewhere today.

Scarlett's brother, Bailey, lived in what could best be described as a hovel. When we arrived there the second time for the day, it was clear someone else had also visited him. Where his house had been closed up earlier, the front door had been kicked in since and the place had been trashed. And Bailey was still nowhere to be seen.

I called Scarlett. "Your brother still isn't home. Do you have any idea where else he might be?"

"He mainly hangs out at a local pub when he's not working, and sometimes he's at his on-off girlfriend's place. I'm not sure if they're together at the moment, though."

"Can you text me those addresses and I'll check them out?"

She agreed and we ended the call.

Griff was poking around in the kitchen and looked up as I entered the small room. "This guy's got a bad addiction. I don't reckon Scarlett's got a chance in hell of helping him kick it."

I had to agree with him. Bailey's kitchen counter was littered with used needles and other shit. Not only was he a junkie, he was a dirty fuck who didn't like to clean up after himself.

My phone began ringing and Griff eyed it. "Jesus, your phone never shuts up."

Blade.

"Tell me this is good news," I said as I answered him.

"Sorry, can't do that." The tense strain in his voice was undeniable – Blade had more bad news for us.

"Fuck," I muttered.

"It's Rogue."

174

The hairs on the back of my neck stood up at the way his words came out. "What?" I urged.

"Harlow asked me to look into him while you were away. She had an off feeling about him and she was right. He's working against you, helping Julio. And on top of that, he's wanted for multiple rapes. Seems he's gotten himself into some shit while he's been away from the club."

My body stilled.

Rogue's with Harlow at the moment.

My mind slammed into my heart and nausea coursed through me. Then the sound of gunfire rang out, and everything blurred as Griff and I battled bullets.

Chapter Thirteen
Harlow

"So, you've told Scott you're pregnant?" Scarlett asked as we loaded the dishwasher in the café kitchen.

"No, not yet," I admitted quietly.

"Shit, girl, when are you going to tell him?"

"I was going to do it last night, but then he came home from your place all stressed and it just didn't feel like the right time to do it."

"I don't think there is a right time for this kind of conversation, except for *as soon as fucking possible*." She stopped what she was doing and stared at me as if she was waiting for me to agree with her.

"I'm honestly going to do it. He's just got so much going on at the moment."

She nodded at me like she didn't believe me, and I was about to defend my decision again, but the sound of Mum coughing from the front of the café stopped me. I headed out to where she stood hunched over, still coughing. She'd been getting progressively worse all day.

"Go home, Mum," I suggested as I rubbed her back. "I'm sorry I gave you a cold, but at least I'm all better, so I can look after the café while you rest."

She coughed one last time before straightening. Nodding, she said, "Thanks, love. Hopefully I'll be better tomorrow."

"Don't come in if you're not. I'll take care of everything."

She took off her apron and hung it up in the kitchen before grabbing her bag and heading out. I gave her a kiss goodbye and told her again not to come in tomorrow if she wasn't up to it. Knowing my mother, though, she'd be in even if she was sick.

"I like your mum," Scarlett said after she'd gone.

"She's a good woman."

The three of us had gotten on really well and the day had flown by with Scarlett helping us. Mum had mentioned that perhaps she might want a part-time job, but I hadn't had time to mention it to her yet. Besides, I

177

wanted to spend more time with her before offering her a job – I wasn't sure whether Scarlett was someone I could spend a lot of time with.

"My mother never gives me the time of day," she blurted while fidgeting with the tea towel. This was the first time she'd shared something personal with me.

"You're not close?"

"No. The only person I'm close to in my family is my brother, and most of the time that's only because I force myself into his life." As she said this, she pulled her phone out and checked for a text from Scott. She'd been checking it religiously since he called about her brother.

"Still no news?"

She shook her head. "Nothing yet."

"Do you want to call Scott and ask him? Maybe he got tied up and forgot to call." I doubted it, but I figured it couldn't hurt.

She tapped her phone against her leg in a nervous type gesture, and then said, "Yeah, I might give him a call."

"Okay, I'll leave you to it."

I headed to the bathroom and gave her some privacy while she phoned Scott. It had been a busy day and I was exhausted. We only had another hour at work and I was clock watching for that minute we could close up shop and go home.

Tonight I will tell Scott.

Even if he's busy with club stuff, I'll make him sit down for a minute so I can tell him.

178

I took my time in the bathroom in case Scarlett had managed to get hold of Scott and when I finished, I wandered back out to the front of the café looking for her. However, she was nowhere to be found, and instead, Rogue came barrelling in through the front door.

"What the fuck is she doing?" he roared, fury plastered across his face.

I shrunk away from him. I'd never seen him so angry. "What is who doing?"

"Don't give me that shit. Scarlett. She just screamed out of here in your car."

Oh shit.

"I was in the bathroom; I didn't realise she had left." A shot of nerves spiked through me and I reached into my back pocket for my phone. I dialled Scott twice, but both times the call went straight to his message bank.

Rogue stared at me while I frantically tried to get hold of Scott. After my second attempt, he said, "He's not answering?"

My heart dropped into my stomach.

This is not good.

I took a step back. "No, but I'll keep trying."

Or maybe I'll try Blade.

As I jabbed at my phone to find Blade's number, Rogue snatched it out of my hands and stomped on it. His dark eyes met mine and he snarled, "There's no point trying Scott again 'cause he's not likely to answer any time soon."

179

My hands madly flailed beside me, searching for a chair to lean on as my legs almost gave way.

No.

Not Scott.

My heart thumped in my chest and I yelled, "What have you done to him?"

This can't be happening.

He laughed and it was the most sinister laugh I'd ever heard. "Scott Cole's getting what he's deserved for a long fucking time, and you, you little bitch, are gonna get what I've been wanting to give you since I fucking met you."

He took a step towards me and I stumbled backwards. My legs were like jelly and didn't want to move. Fear had taken over my body completely – fear for Scott's life and fear for what I knew Rogue wanted to do to me.

"No!" I screamed and turned to run into the kitchen. We had a back door and if I could just get to that, I could get outside and run for help.

Even though my legs didn't want to move, I forced them to. The adrenaline flowing through my body helped me make it to the back door, but the door was locked.

Oh my God.

No. No. No.

My fear roared in my ears and I gritted my teeth against the nausea forcing itself upon me.

Even though I knew Rogue was right behind me, I turned. I had to. The key for the door was in my bag and I had to at least try to get it.

He stood right behind me when I turned, and because I'd anticipated that, I kneed him in the balls and shoved him hard so he stumbled back.

As he screamed obscenities at me, I hurried to my bag, but then I had another idea. I decided to keep heading for the front door instead of fumbling in my bag for the back door key.

"You fucking bitch!" he shouted and I realised he was close again.

Shit.

I was halfway to the front door when his hand latched onto my shoulder and he yanked me back. His strength was too great for me to struggle against and I fell back into his grip.

"You're gonna regret messing with me, Harlow." His breath crawled across my face as he pressed his mouth close to my cheek.

No asshole, you're going to regret messing with me.

Thank God Scott taught me some self-defence.

I dropped my weight and then aimed my elbow up and back at his head. At the same time, I stomped on his feet and then rotated out of his hold. I kicked him hard in the balls again and when he doubled over in pain, I took a step back and kicked up under his face as hard as I could which caused him a great deal of pain.

He held his face as he stumbled around yelling at me. When I was satisfied I'd slowed him down enough, I turned to run as fast as I could away from the café to go in search of help.

As I turned, a car's brakes screeched outside and in the next moment, something smashed through the window.

Flames came alive right in front of me and I screamed out as they licked my arm.

The glass in another one of our windows smashed and an explosion of fire almost deafened me.

And then everything went black.

Chapter Fourteen
Scott

I'm going to fucking kill Rogue.

I stalked into the hospital and up to the room where I'd been told Harlow was. We'd received the call nearly an hour ago that there'd been a fire at her mum's café, and the traffic had been a bitch, so a trip that should have taken me half an hour at the most had taken me almost double the time.

When I finally found her room, and saw her awake and talking to her mother, I let out a long breath of relief. I hadn't realised I'd been holding it in.

She turned to look at me, and gave me a smile. "Hey, baby."

I sat on the edge of her bed and took hold of her hand. "Fuck, you had me worried." I was pretty sure the minute I'd heard the words 'molotov cocktail', my heart had stopped beating.

"I was just lucky one of my customers turned up in time to drag me out of the café before I got burnt."

Guilt that she'd been affected by Storm business washed through me. Raking my fingers through my hair, I said, "I'm so sorry this happened to you." I turned to Cheryl. "And to your café, too."

Cheryl nodded. "It's not your fault, Scott."

Anger punched through me - at this, and at everything threatening Storm. My gut twisted with that anger and for a moment, I felt like nothing we were doing was working. One step forward and two fucking steps back was what it felt like.

Harlow squeezed my hand and centred me again. I breathed through it and focused my attention back on her.

"Rogue tried to attack me, Scott," she said quietly, almost as if she was afraid of my reaction. "He is not a good man."

"Why didn't you tell me about your problems with him?"

"I didn't want to burden you with it so I spoke to Blade about it. He's investigating Rogue for us."

"Yeah, he told me today. You don't need to worry about Rogue anymore, sweetheart, okay?" God, it killed me that she'd had to even worry about him in the first place. All I wanted was for Harlow to be safe, and I'd fucking put danger right in her path.

Her eyes widened. "Did he die in that fire? I thought he got out, too."

I placed my finger to her lips. "All you need to know is that he won't ever get in your way again. I want you to promise me something, though."

"What?"

"Promise me you'll always come to me with this kind of stuff in the future. I need to know any concern you ever have. I need to know that you're safe at all times."

"I promise."

I bent and pressed a kiss to her forehead. "Thank fuck."

She bit her lip as I straightened, and I knew she had something to tell me – Harlow only bit her lip that way when she was keeping something from me.

"What?" I asked.

Her mouth curled up in a smile and her hand rested on my forearm. "I'm pregnant," she whispered, and for the second time today, my heart skipped a beat.

185

And then it sped up.

"The baby's okay after the fire?" Jesus, I'd torture Rogue before killing him if the baby had been harmed. Fuck it, maybe I'd torture him anyway.

"Yes, thank God. The doctor just wants to keep me in overnight to make sure."

Cassie interrupted us at that moment. "Oh my God, Harlow! Are you okay?" She came flying through the door, almost knocking me over in her haste to get to Harlow.

I stood and gave them some space. Cassie was good for Harlow, and although Harlow had pushed Cassie away a little over the past few months, her friend had always been there for her. I never begrudged them time together.

My phone sounded with a text.

Griff: Ward 5A Bed 6

I shoved my phone back in my pocket and cut in on Harlow's conversation with Cassie. "I'm going to let you girls have some time while I take care of something. I'll be back soon."

Harlow frowned. "Is everything okay?"

"Yeah, baby, I'll be less than half an hour and then I'm here all night."

No fucking way am I not staying all night.

186

She gave me a smile. "Can you please get me a drink while you're gone?"

"Coffee? Tea?"

"Surprise me."

I brushed a kiss across her lips and lingered there for a moment. "I love you," I murmured.

"Love you, too," she whispered. Her words meant more to me than anything in that moment.

She still loves me regardless of the fact my club almost got her killed.

As I walked towards the elevator, I allowed the anger I'd kept in check to pump through me and clenched my fists as I imagined what I was about to do.

I had two reasons for breathing in life and when someone messed with either of those, I'd spend my days making sure they never had the chance to do it again.

★★★

I stood in the doorway and watched as Rogue slept. Hospital life carried on around us, but my mind filtered the activity out as I focused all my attention on the man who'd messed with my woman and my club.

My boot sounded on the floor as I took a step towards him, and his eyes blinked open at the noise.

Lines creased his forehead as he frowned. "Scott?" he asked, his voice thick with confusion.

"Yeah, motherfucker, I'm alive even though you worked to make sure I wasn't. Griff's still breathing, too, but you'll see that for yourself any minute now." I had no proof he was behind Griff and I getting shot at earlier, but the look that crossed his face was all the evidence I needed.

When he didn't say anything, I asked, "Why?"

"Why, what?"

My anger flared at his continued charade. "Why the fuck did you turn on us?"

He stared at me for a few moments, hedging his bets by the look of it, before finally spitting out, "Marcus was right about you when he said you had a God complex. You shouldn't have killed him. You shouldn't be the fucking president of Storm!"

"I didn't fuckin' kill him."

"That's a lie."

Griff's voice sounded behind me as he clicked the door shut. "No, it's not. Scott did not kill Marcus."

Rogue's gaze flicked to Griff. "You should both be dead for what you've done to the club."

"What the fuck have we done that's so bad? If anything, we've made it better," I threw back.

"Marcus had a plan for the club, a plan that involved drugs and a whole lot of cash, and you two fucked with that plan. You fucked with my chance at a happy future."

Clarity hit me. "So this all comes down to money."

"Money and fucking happiness."

I lowered my face closer to his. "There's something to be said for clean cash, Rogue...cash that doesn't hurt people. Marcus never gave a shit about whether his actions hurt other people, but Griff and I do. Storm will *never* fuckin' deal in drugs again."

Griff cut in. "So, you figured you'd feed Julio information about the club and let him take us down?"

Hatred burned in Rogue's eyes. "I gave him what he needed to get to you two. He was supposed to take both of you out, as well as the other club members I'd identified as being opposed to drugs. I wouldn't think for one second that just because you're still breathing, you're safe. Julio intends to control this state. Anyone who gets in his way will be taken care of." He paused for a moment before adding, "And that bitch of yours sure did feel good warming my bed while you were away." Another lie. They just seemed to fall from his mouth.

I clenched my jaw as I punched his face.

Motherfucker.

"I'm really fuckin' happy that fire didn't kill you, and that one of Harlow's customers pulled you from it," I snarled.

He spat blood from his mouth. "Fuck you."

I punched him again. As the satisfaction coursed through me, I yelled, "No, fuck *you*!"

"We need to hurry this along, brother," Griff warned.

I nodded. "Yeah."

189

I yanked one of the pillows out from under Rogue's head, enjoying the fear I saw in his eyes. His arms lashed out at me, trying to halt my progress, but nothing would stop me from this. When I finally had the pillow over his face, I pressed down hard while Griff restrained his arms. His body fought death and his grunts composed the soundtrack to his demise, but all I heard was the sweet, sweet music of triumph.

Finally, something is going our way.

As I eyed the drinks available in the hospital café, Griff said, "Blood is about to be shed, isn't it?"

I grabbed a can of coke, a bottle of orange juice, a carton of strawberry milk and a green smoothie before answering him. Meeting his gaze, I said, "A *lot* of fuckin' blood."

"You thirsty, brother?" he said as he jerked his chin at the drinks in my arms.

"Not me. Harlow. She didn't tell me what she wanted so I'll just get her everything she loves."

A smile twitched at his lips. "When are you gonna marry that woman?"

"As soon as I can fuckin' perfect the proposal."

He laughed. "Four words, brother, that's all it takes. I'm sure you can manage that."

I paid for the drinks and as we walked towards the elevator, Griff's phone rang. He took the call and I watched as a frown replaced the smile on his face.

When he ended the call, he said, "That was J. Nash and Velvet were just run off the road. They're not hurt - thank fuck they were in her car and not on his bike - but Nash is fired up and ready to take on Julio. J's trying to talk him down and get him to wait for us. And Scarlett turned up at the clubhouse, minus her brother. Apparently she got word from him, though, and he's left town and is okay."

I thought about that for a minute and then balanced Harlow's drinks in my arms so I could pull out my phone. I dialled a number and when he answered, I said, "We're gonna need your help, King."

"I'm one step ahead of you, brother. We'll be there tomorrow."

I didn't even ask him how he knew we needed him. King had his sources and if he wanted to share that information with me, he would in his own time. I simply said, "Thank you."

"King's on his way?" Griff asked when I'd finished my call.

"Yeah. Someone, somewhere, knows something, and I'm hoping we're about to get to the fuckin' bottom of this shit."

"You and me both. It's time Storm had some good shit happen. The last couple of years have been hell."

When the elevator hit Harlow's level, we stepped out and almost ran into Blade who was on his phone, pacing in front of the lifts. He spun around and ended his call as he met my gaze.

"Julio's gone to ground," he stated.

"How? We've got Gunnar watching him," Griff said.

"Someone drugged Gunnar. I just sent one of my guys around to check in with him and he was just coming to. Julio's cleared everything out of his place and I can't find anyone who knows where he is."

"Jesus! Can this day get any worse?" My temper exploded.

"Also, your mother needs to see you."

"Why the fuck is my mother contacting *you* about needing to see *me*?"

His brows lifted. "Apparently, you don't answer her calls."

Fuck.

I *had* been ignoring her today.

He continued, "She says it can't wait."

So much for spending the whole night with Harlow.

Chapter Fifteen
Scott

"Is Harlow okay?"

Irritation at being dragged away from her, and a need to get back to her as soon as possible, caused me to snap at my mother when she didn't deserve it. "She's fine. What was so important that I had to come right now?" Harlow had understood, but I didn't feel the same way.

Mum squared her shoulders and placed her hands on her hips. "Don't take that shitty tone of voice with me, Scott. I would not have asked you to come if it wasn't important."

I forced out a breath and tried to calm down. "Sorry. Today's been hard, but you didn't deserve that." I paused as the emotions running through me came to the surface. My voice softened as I added, "Harlow is pregnant again."

Her eyes widened and a smile spread across her face. "That's the best news I've heard for a long time!"

Nodding, I said, "Yeah...I'm concerned, though."

"Why?"

I sat on her couch and rested my elbows on my knees. My muscles had knotted in my shoulders and back, and I dropped my head forward to stretch my neck. Looking back up at her, I laid out my fears. "Harlow told me she didn't want to try for a baby again just yet. I'm worried this is too soon for her when she's still trying to work through her grief. She's come so far and I don't want her to ever go back to where she was."

Mum sat next to me and placed her hand on my shoulder. "Scott, sometimes what we think will be the worst thing for us, turns out to be exactly what we need. I've been keeping an eye on Harlow and I think things have changed for her. I think she's stronger now and has the mental tools to cope with whatever happens. Amongst other things she's been doing that helped, you going away was good for her."

"Why?"

"It forced her to take some responsibility on again, and it also gave her something besides herself to think about.

She was busy looking after Lisa and Michelle, as well as the café with her mum, and trying to help Wilder out."

I thought I'd noticed a change in Harlow, but I figured I'd been seeing something that perhaps wasn't there. *What I wanted to see.* But maybe Mum was right.

Pressing my back against the couch, I said, "I hope you're right. And I hope to fuck we don't lose this baby." I drummed my fingers on my leg and did my best to ignore the tightness in my chest. *We can't lose this one.*

"If you lose another child, you'll face that together. You're an amazing man and I'm so proud of the way you've stood by Harlow. Even though your father set the worst example of how to be a man and a husband, you've figured out how to do it right, and Harlow is very lucky to have you." Her eyes misted over as she took a breath. When she spoke again, her voice cracked as she felt her way through her words. "I'm so sorry for allowing your father to remain a part of our family while you were growing up. I wish I'd done better and given you and Madison the kind of father you both deserved. But I can't go back; all I can do is be there for you now, whenever and however you need me."

I took all her words in, hearing her for what felt like the first time in a long time. I'd shut her out over the last year, but it was time to let her back in. Mum had suffered at the hands of my father for so long; she didn't need to keep hurting.

It's time to put our family back together.

195

Reaching for her hand, I murmured, "When you know better, you do better, right?"

Tears slid down her face as she nodded. "Yes," she whispered.

We sat in silence for a while, lost in our own thoughts. A man who only cared about himself had screwed up our family from the beginning. I would build us back up and give us the opportunity to be the strong family we always should have been.

Eventually, Mum wiped her tears and squeezed my hand. Smiling, she said softly, "I've got someone who wants to see you."

I frowned as she stood and left the room. When she returned a minute later with a red-headed man, I stood and jerked my chin at him. "Blue." *Uncle Dan.* The key to understanding so damn much that we'd struggled with for so long.

He nodded. "Scott."

"You're finally coming home? Or just visiting?"

Blue smiled at Mum before turning back to me. "I'm moving back to Brisbane. Finally."

I watched their interaction closely, and anger at my father roared through me again. He'd done this – he'd broken a brother and sister apart, all for his own gain. Not that I knew the full story, but I knew enough to know that.

Regret, nostalgia and hope circled the three of us as the significance of this day was acknowledged. "What

196

happened all those years ago, Blue? How the hell did my father force you to agree to leave town?"

His chest rose and fell hard before he exhaled a long breath. Nodding at the couch, he suggested, "Take a seat, son. This is a long story."

Son.

I had good memories of Blue. He'd always been a strong male presence in my life. Dad hadn't wanted us to spend a lot of time with him, but Mum had snuck visits in when she could. Looking back now, I realised it was thanks to Blue that I'd learnt how to treat a woman right. He'd had a long-time girlfriend who he'd cherished, and I'd watched them for years, taking in the way he showed his love for her.

"Your father and I always had a hard relationship. I chose not to join Storm even though our family had a long history of membership with my father and his father before him. Dad supported my decision not to join, but Marcus belittled me for it. I had little respect for Marcus, but Sharon wanted him in her life, so I stood by her choice and watched out for her. Then I met Miranda and I knew she'd be the woman I would spend the rest of my life with. We never married, but we didn't need that. What we did need, though, was for Marcus to leave her alone..." He stopped talking and swallowed hard as his hands clenched.

My gut churned. I sensed he was about to tell me something ugly about my father. As if there weren't enough ugly truths about him already.

I was right.

Blue's eyes met mine and the pain I saw there hit me in the chest. When I flicked my gaze to Mum, I took in her ashen face. This wasn't going to be easy to hear, but it had to be said. I wasn't sure how I knew, but the understanding sat deep in my soul that we needed this out on the table in order for us all to move forward.

Blue cleared his throat. "I've already told your mother, so she already knows this." He paused and I nodded. *Tell me.* "Marcus wanted a relationship with Miranda, but she said no. She never told me because she didn't want to hurt your mother or me with the revelation. He tried to sleep with her a few times and she continued to say no, but one night when I was out of town, he forced himself on her. He raped her and then threatened her so she wouldn't ever tell anyone."

My mouth turned dry and nausea rolled through my stomach.

My father had more evil inside him than I'd ever realised.

Mum wept beside me while I balled my fists. The need to lash out was strong. I wanted to punch my anger at my father out of my body, but I controlled that need, and waited to hear what else Blue had to say.

198

"I never knew all this until very recently when I went through her journals. I kept them all these years after her death, but never worked up the courage to read them until now."

"She died of a drug overdose, right?" I said.

"Yes. After she was raped, she turned to drugs to deal with the pain. I could never understand what led her to the drugs, but it all makes sense now."

"How does this all fit in with you leaving town?"

"I never knew why she did drugs, but I always knew she was getting them off Storm. Off your father. After she overdosed, I went to the police to try and help them bring Marcus down. I worked with them for a while, and in the course of that, I stumbled across the fact your father killed a cop who had blackmailed him into snitching on Sydney Storm. Apparently, the cop discovered Marcus had killed a biker from another club and used that information to force him to give them details on drug deals Sydney was involved in. The VP of Sydney and two other members ended up doing time after Marcus gave the cop details of their activities. When the VP went to jail, Marcus panicked and killed the cop so Sydney would never know it was him. After I discovered this, I blackmailed him myself – told him to get Storm out of drugs altogether, or I would tell Sydney what he'd done. I didn't want you kids to deal in drugs, and neither did your grandfather. This was my one opportunity to put an end to that era of Storm."

199

And all the pieces fall together.

"So you had to leave town or Marcus would have killed you," I said as I pieced it all together.

He nodded. "Yes, and I had to keep moving around over the years because Marcus had his feelers everywhere. That Adelaide President was in his pocket and came close to finding me a few times."

I scowled. "I don't trust that asshole."

Before Blue could say anything further, a knock at Mum's back door cut through our conversation.

"You expecting someone?" I asked as I stood.

They shook their heads, so I left them to go and see who it was. I pulled my gun out, ready for any possibility.

The tall cop who'd stood at my front door the other day, now stood in front of me at Mum's door. "What the fuck do you want at this time of night?" I demanded as I shoved my gun away.

"Blue here?" he enquired.

"What the fuck?" I was completely confused now.

Blue joined us. "Let him in, Scott. Carter's working with me on this."

Carter?

Working together.

What the fuck?

I spun around to face Blue. "What the hell is going on?"

Carter pushed past me, shutting the door as he went. "I'll tell you what the fuck *I've* got going on," he

200

muttered, meeting my gaze. "I've just come from the hospital where I have a dead informant lying in one their beds. You know anything about that?"

"Fuck, did you kill Rogue?" Blue asked, his voice strained.

I eyed the cop, not willing to admit anything in front of him.

Carter raised his brows and said, "I reckon he did, so there goes our lead on Bourne."

I held up my hand. "Wait one fuckin' minute. Can one of you tell me what the fuck you're talking about?"

They exchanged a look before Blue finally shed some light on what they were up to. "Carter is Miranda's brother. I asked for his help when I learnt Marcus was working with Bourne to find me and also to get Storm back into the drugs. We've been working together to bring Bourne down, but the asshole covers his tracks so damn well, we've struggled."

"Up until now," Carter drawled. "Rogue was wanted in Queensland on some charges and I was cutting a deal with him. In exchange for information on Bourne, I would work to drop some of the charges."

"Rogue was working with Bourne?" I asked.

"Rogue was working with everyone, Scott. Whoever paid him got the information. He didn't care who he told what to, so long as he got cash for it," Blue explained.

"Fuck," I muttered, stunned at his double crossing. "So you're after Bourne, not Julio?"

201

"Bourne wants Julio dead. He wants control of Julio's territory. I want them both dealt with. My investigation of Bourne has been on my own time because it's in another State, but now that Julio is dealing in Queensland, I'm investigating him on work time, and am hoping to get to Bourne that way," Carter explained.

"Jesus, it's a fuckin' mess in my head at the moment," I said. "All this double crossing and secrets." I eyed Carter. "Why are you telling me all this? Aren't you investigating me, too?"

Carter ran his fingers through his hair and sighed. "I'm going to be real honest with you, Cole. Your father was a piece of shit and when he died, I celebrated with drinks. It was one of the happiest days of my life, knowing that the man responsible for my sister's death was dead. Then I got lumped with fucking investigating that death when Rogue turned up with his bullshit information, accusing you of killing Marcus. My partner is all over that investigation, but I'm not. Now that Rogue is dead, I'll be doing my best to shut that down. For all I care, you could have tortured your father for a year before killing him and I wouldn't give a shit. And as long as Storm keeps its hands clean of drugs, I don't care what else you do. But next time you want to suffocate one of my informants, give me a head's up, so I can get the information out of them that I need before they die."

I wasn't sure what to make of him, and I sure as shit wasn't admitting to anything, but I was ecstatic to hear he'd be ending the investigation into Marcus's death. The less I had to worry about, the better.

"Where does this leave us?" I asked, ready to get back to Harlow, but needing to know what lay ahead.

"As I suspect you already know, Julio has gone missing From what I have been told, Bourne's left Adelaide and is heading to Brisbane, but he's not here yet. I want you to let me know if you hear from Bourne. I believe he's coming here to kill Julio, so I need to know when he hits town."

I held his gaze and lied to his face. "I'll be in touch if I hear anything, but for now, I need to get back to the hospital."

No fucking way was I giving up Bourne. To do that would mean also giving up my opportunity to kill Julio, and I wasn't giving that up for anyone.

That honour would be mine.

Chapter Sixteen
Scott

I stared out the window of the clubhouse office and contemplated everything I knew, which seemed to change so often I wasn't sure what to think.

I'd spent the night with Harlow at the hospital last night and done my best to focus on her and put what Carter and Blue had told me out of my mind for the night. The doctors had agreed to let her go home this morning and once I'd gotten her home and settled, she'd told me to leave and take care of Storm business.

I loved that woman.

I loved that she gave me the space to do what she knew I needed to do.

I'd been at the clubhouse for the past hour with Griff, J and Nash, going over scenarios for how to deal with Julio. We'd worked out a plan, but then Carter had called to let me know four of Julio's men had been found dead. That information confused the fuck out of us.

I turned to face them. "Who would be killing Julio's guys? It doesn't make any sense."

"I don't get it, either," J replied, looking as confused as I felt.

The rumble of pipes caught our attention and I turned back to the window to see five bikes making their way into our driveway.

"King's arrived," I said. "Maybe he can shed some light on this."

I sure as fuck hoped so.

We made our way outside and watched as he walked our way with a grim look on his face. He'd brought Kick, Hyde, Nitro and Devil with him. His go-to guys when shit was going down.

He knows something.

"How's Harlow?" he asked.

"She's doing good today."

He nodded. "Thank fuck for that."

"Tell me what you know," I threw out, fed up with not knowing what he knew. Someone had clearly told him we needed help, and I wanted to know who it was.

205

He slapped me on the back and walked me inside. "I can't. Not yet, anyway. But as soon as I talk to my source and confirm some things, you'll be the first to know."

"So, what's the plan?" Kick asked.

"Before we go through that, I discovered last night that Marcus *was* the one who snitched on your club ten years ago," I said to King.

"Who confirmed that?" he asked.

"My uncle."

"Good to know, but I wish to fuck I'd known before he died. We would have enjoyed the payback."

"Yeah, you and me both, brother," I muttered, thinking about what I now knew of my father. He would have deserved everything King would have done to him.

Griff stepped in, eager to get today underway. Fuck, we all were. "Julio's gone into hiding so we need to flush him out, and then we want him dead. Fucking around trying to get shit smoothed over before we kill him is holding us up too much, so we'll just deal with the fallout once it's done."

"To be honest," I added, "I think his crew will fall apart once he's dead anyway. Bourne seemed certain there would be a lot of blowback, but I don't see it, or at least I don't think it would be anything we all couldn't handle now that you guys are here and Blade's guys are on board. And I just got word that four of Julio's guys have turned up dead, so we now have less to deal with anyway."

King frowned. "Any idea who killed them?"

"No. It's odd," I said.

He pulled his phone out. "I'll make a call; I may know who it is." He walked outside to make his call in private.

While he was gone, we divided up the list of places to check for Julio between everyone we had. Blade's men were also out looking, and I hoped to have Julio by the end of the day.

As everyone began breaking away to head out on their search, King came back inside. "I'm gonna go see this guy and try to get the information out of him. As soon as I have any new info, I'll call you."

Griff and I watched him go. "Jesus, you'd think he could share what he suspected with us," Griff muttered, clearly as frustrated as I was.

"You'd think so, but he always has kept his cards close to his chest, I guess." I stretched the kinks out of my back as I thought about Harlow. Once we had Julio and all this crap sorted out, I was making good on my promise of a proposal. But fuck if she thought I would wait to get that ring on her finger. As soon as she said yes, I'd be walking her down the aisle and calling her Mrs Cole.

"I'm just gonna check in with Harlow and make sure she's okay before we head out," I said as I grabbed my phone and walked out to the clubhouse bar.

She answered on the first ring. "Hey, baby. Is everything going okay?" I heard the concern in her voice. My mission today was to wipe that concern from her mind.

"It's all good here. You feeling okay?"

"Yeah, I'm good. Mum and I are just going over the café insurance paperwork, and Scarlett is here giving Wilder a hard time. It's kinda fun to watch."

I'd asked Wilder to keep an eye on them today. I was kicking myself that I hadn't asked him to watch out for her all this time, rather than getting Rogue to do it.

"I'm just a phone call away if you need me, sweetheart."

"I know," she said, softly. "I love you, Scott."

And there was my reason for everything.

Her faith.

Her trust.

Her love.

"I love you, too. I'll call you in a few hours and check in again."

After the call, I was even more determined to find Julio and right all the wrongs we had at the moment. And regardless of all the shit Storm had been through over the last couple of years, I would build it back up to be the strong club it had always been.

"You ready to go?" Griff asked a few minutes later when I found him in the office.

I nodded. "Let's do this, brother."

The clubhouse was eerily quiet as we walked out of the office. It was unusual for there to be no one around, but between sending members out to search for Julio and

208

others out to keep an eye on our families, there wasn't anyone left to stay at the clubhouse.

As Griff pulled on the front door to exit, Julio Rivera stumbled in.

I knew it was him because I'd looked at enough photos of the man that I'd be able to identify him even if I was drunk.

Griff and I both pulled our guns out and aimed them at him, but he didn't even try to fight us. He simply held his hands up in surrender.

What the hell?

I pressed my gun against his forehead. "You picked a good place to come, motherfucker. We've got the fuckin' welcome mat out for you today."

"I've got information for you, Mr Cole, and I would suggest you don't kill me because you are going to want this information."

"I'm not sure what information you could have that I would want. Really, at this point, all I want is for you to stop breathing." I grabbed his hand and yanked him past me so I could walk behind him. Once I had my gun pressed to his back, I ordered, "Walk!"

We led him out to one of the back rooms of the clubhouse and once Griff had him tied to a chair, I punched him a few times in an effort to get out the anger burning through me. He'd fucked us over too many times, and I had to restrain myself from punching him until he was unconscious.

209

His head lolled to the side and blood dripped down from his face onto the floor. He spat out the blood pooling in his mouth and looked back up at me. "I'm done," he forced out on a heave.

"What the fuck do you mean by that?" Griff demanded.

"Bourne's threatened to kill my sister if I don't give him my territory. I'm walking away from everything."

"Jesus Christ, you two are a fuckin' class act. I don't believe you, asshole. I don't believe a word that comes out of your mouth!" I yelled.

Griff's shoulders were wound tight with tension, and he'd been holding back, but he reached the end of his control. He punched Julio, over and over, until Julio's face was unrecognisable.

"Feel good?" I asked.

His head jerked around and his eyes found mine.

Wild.

Feral.

Griff had so much darkness in him that he concealed from the world under a carefully constructed mask, but in that moment, I saw it. Loud and clear.

He took a deep breath. "Yeah," he grunted.

Julio mumbled something, but his lips were so swollen he could hardly get the words out. Griff grabbed his hair and yanked his head back. "What did you say?" he barked.

210

Julio attempted to open his lips, but struggled. His breathing was laboured and it was clear he was in a great deal of pain.

Good.

He mumbled again, and again we couldn't make out what he said.

I clenched my hands, wanting desperately to take that last breath from him, while also wanting to drag his pain and suffering out.

Griff yanked his head again. Harder. "Speak so we can understand you, asshole!"

Julio's face contorted in agony when Griff punched him again.

"Bourne," he mumbled, but not so much that we couldn't make out that word. He tried to open his mouth again, but only ended up pushing out a cry of pain before closing it again. His breathing slowed and I wondered if he was about to lose consciousness. And then he managed to force out more words. "He's...not...who...he...says..." – he coughed – "...he...is..."

And then his head dropped forward and he passed out.

Griff turned and punched the wall before looking back at me. "What the fuck does *that* mean?"

"Jesus...your guess is as good as mine."

"I wanted to kill the asshole, but now I'm thinking we might need to let him live for a bit longer."

My phone rang.

Blade.

"Tell me you've got information that will help us. We've got Julio here and he's just told us some shit about Bourne not being who he says he is, but then he passed out, so we have no clue what he meant by that," I said, answering the call.

"Bourne *isn't* who you think he is, Scott. I've just discovered that Julio actually works for Bourne."

"You've gotta be fuckin' kidding me." All my conversations with Bourne filtered back through my mind, none of them making any sense now.

"They go way back. Bourne had an affair with Julio's sister when they were younger and they have a child together. Bourne put Julio as the face of his operation and let everyone think Julio was in charge. Once he had South Australia under his full control, he sent Julio to take over Queensland, but somewhere along the way, Bourne decided he wanted Julio out. Problem was, he couldn't just get rid of him because Julio's men were loyal to him and if they knew Bourne killed Julio, they would retaliate against him."

"And that's where we came in...Bourne was using us to do his dirty work," I said as it began to make sense.

"There's something else."

"What?"

"Bourne wants control of your club so he can run the drugs through it. He wants you and anyone else in his way dead. And he's in Brisbane now, ready to make that happen. He already took out some of Julio's men earlier; it seems he's on a mission to get shit done. You need to make sure everyone is locked up tight while we find Bourne."

"I'm on it."

When I ended the call, I said to Griff, "Call your family, brother, and tell them to lock up tight. Bourne's been playing us and is now after us. I'm gonna call Harlow and then I'll fill you in."

He nodded and we both made the calls we needed to.

"Hey, baby," Harlow answered a moment later.

"Harlow, I need you to make sure the house is locked up and you stay alert. There's a guy looking for me and I'm concerned he may come there." I tried to keep my voice free of the tension I was feeling, but I needed her to take this threat seriously, so I was firm.

"Okay...how worried should I be?" She sounded like she was biting her lip.

"You've got Wilder there with you, and I'm going to try to send someone else as well."

"I think we'll be okay. One of your Adelaide guys just arrived to help Wilder, so -"

I cut her off, frantic to know the name of the guy. "Who?"

"I'm pretty sure Wilder called him Bourne."

Icy fear slid down my spine as my world spun.

I can't lose her.

I can't lose our baby.

213

"I'm coming now, Harlow." I hung up without waiting for her reply.

I promised her I would always protect her.

I promised her I would marry her.

I intended to keep those promises.

Chapter Seventeen
Harlow

That was odd.

I stared at my phone after Scott hung up on me. "Weird," I said as I placed my phone on the table.

"What?" Scarlett asked as she made coffee for Wilder and Bourne.

I frowned as I recalled the abrupt way Scott ended our call. "Scott kinda just hung up on me. It's so out of character for him to do that."

She shrugged. "Seems like he's got a lot of pressure on him at the moment."

"Yeah, you're right." He really did. But my man knew how to handle his shit, so I was still a little thrown by what he'd just done.

"I want to apologise again for running out on you yesterday." She'd already apologised twice so there really was no need.

"Scarlett, even if you hadn't run out, Rogue would probably still have shown his true colours, and the fire would have still happened, so none of it was your fault. Okay?" I'd seen a whole new caring side to her, but she needed to listen to what I was saying and stop saying sorry.

"Okay," she murmured.

I was about to say something else when a fight broke out on the back veranda. Wilder yelled something at Bourne who then shouted back. And then it sounded like a scuffle and perhaps a punch up.

Scarlett and I hurried outside to see what was going on. Just as I exited the house through the back door, Bourne knocked Wilder unconscious with a punch to the head.

"What are you doing?" I screamed, panic bubbling up.

Bourne's eyes came to mine, and in that instant, I realised he was not a good man. He pointed a gun at us, and barked, "Get the fuck inside."

"Jesus," Scarlett muttered, "Do you attract assholes or something?"

"It would appear so," I agreed as we walked back inside. I fought to remain calm on the outside, because I refused to show him any fear, but on the inside, I was scrambling to come up with an escape plan.

Bourne had already been inside when he first arrived, so he knew the layout of the house. "In the lounge room," he ordered, and we did what he said.

As he moved to make sure the door and windows were locked, my hands turned sweaty and my heart raced.

Not again.

Being locked in here with him caused memories from yesterday to flash through my mind and I tried to hold back the feelings of nausea.

I need to fight him.

"What do you want from us?" I demanded to know.

"I want to make Scott Cole hurt. I want him to bleed his pain. And I figure the best way to do that is to take the one thing he treasures the most in the world away from him."

Dread sliced its way through me.

He's going to kill me.

Scott can't save me now.

My fear paralysed me and I stood rooted to the spot when what I should have been doing was formulating a plan to get out of here.

"Fuck you!" Scarlett screamed as she lunged at him.

Unprepared for her attack, he stumbled back as she lashed out at him with her arms and legs. She clawed and

217

kicked him, and for a moment there, I thought she might have a chance against him, but in the end his strength outweighed hers, and he pushed her off.

When she landed on her ass on the floor, he threatened her, "Do that again, bitch, and I'll kill you first."

Oh, God. He's going to kill both of us.

She spat at him, and he hissed his anger at her while bending over and punching her in the face. I watched in horror as he hit her hard, causing her blood, bruises and pain.

I need to distract him.

"Why do you hate Scott so much?" I begged to know while I continued to think of a way out.

His crazy eyes sought mine. "That motherfucker destroyed nearly everything I've worked for over the years. I had it all mapped out, and Marcus went along with it, and then Scott came along and got rid of Marcus and refused to honour the deal I had with Storm. So now I'm going to take it all back and I'm going to take his club, too."

"Are you deluded?" He had to be. To take Storm, he'd have to kill nearly every member because I was pretty sure they weren't about to just hand it over to him.

He slapped me and the sting of his palm radiated pain down my face. "The only person here who is deluded is you, bitch, if you think you're going to make it out of here alive."

I decided to try and call his bluff. "Scott's on his way, you know. He just rang me and said he knew you were in town and that you would be coming to the house. He knows you're working against him."

His body stilled, but only for a moment. "You're full of shit."

Yes. But it's worth a shot.

"No, I'm not." I stood straighter, challenging him.

He advanced on me, his face a mask of rage. "Don't fucking lie to me!" He towered over me and I shrunk a little. Bourne was a large man, and I had no doubt that if he wanted to, he could take me out with very little effort.

I had to be all in or all out. Shaking my head, I said, "I'm not lying. Call him and suss him out if you think I'm full of shit." *Anything to stall him.*

Staring at me for a long moment, it seemed like he finally decided I might be telling the truth. He pulled out his phone, but right before he could make the call, a loud banging sound came from the back of the house.

Bourne's head snapped up and he shoved his gun in my face. "Stay here."

I nodded my agreement as I gulped back my fear. "I will." My shaky voice seemed to please him and he grunted as he stalked away from me.

My legs collapsed underneath me and I let myself fall onto the couch.

Please let that be Scott.

219

"What the fuck?" Bourne yelled in the kitchen, and I prayed again that it was Scott.

"You didn't expect me, did you?" It wasn't Scott, but I was pretty sure I'd heard that voice before, even though I couldn't place it.

"This has nothing to do with you, King," Bourne raged.

"I'd say it has everything to do with me considering I'm the fucking president of the mother chapter."

"You don't want to mess with me," Bourne threatened.

"Fuck, Bourne, how dumb are you? Your ego is about ten sizes too big for you, and that right there is your main problem. Come and play in my playground with the big boys and you'll see how truly little you are. Only reason I haven't dealt with you yet was that I had other shit to take care of for my own club. But I was hardly going to let Scott deal with you when I wanted the satisfaction of slicing the neck of the man who tried to double cross me."

I stood in the doorway between the lounge room and the kitchen and watched their interaction.

Bourne's eyes widened at King's statement. "How...how did - "

King cut him off. "How did I know you double crossed me? I told you, I play with the big boys, and not much gets past us. I've got contacts everywhere and they kept me informed on what you were up to." He leaned in close to Bourne. "I fucking run half of Sydney's drugs and I've actually got a good relationship with the crew that run

220

the other half. We don't take kindly to men who try and steal that shit away from us." His gaze flicked to me and I flinched under it. King oozed darkness. "I also don't fucking like it when you threaten women. That deserves a little extra pain."

I watched as King pulled his knife out and stabbed at Bourne's dick.

Oh, God.

My hand flew to my mouth as Bourne's blood-curdling scream filled the house. His face scrunched up in pain and he bent at the stomach as blood soaked through his jeans.

I experienced a mixture of horror and satisfaction, and it felt wrong to be kind of satisfied at his pain, but after being threatened by two men in the last two days, I was all for them hurting.

King grabbed hold of the back of Bourne's neck and dragged his head back up. He held him so that his neck was exposed and I sucked in a breath when he placed the knife blade against his skin.

Running the blade lightly across his neck, he drew a small amount of blood. "Did I ever tell you how much I love the sight of blood? Other people's blood. That shit turns me on." He pressed harder against Bourne's neck, drawing more blood this time. "Fuck, I could cut patterns on skin for hours."

Bourne whimpered under King's knife, and that only served to excite King more while he continued to draw blood.

221

And then King's phone rang, and it seemed to jolt him from his blood lust. "Fuck," he muttered. Eying me, he asked, "Anything you wanna say to him before I kill him?"

I pulled my shit together and closed the distance between us. Looking King in the eyes, even though he scared the hell out of me, I said, "Thank you, there is something I want to say."

His mouth spread into a smile. Lifting his chin at Bourne, he said, "Go ahead, gorgeous. Have at him."

I turned to Bourne and slapped his face. Hard. Twice. "Fuck you, asshole, and the horse you rode in on."

King's smile twitched and I was certain he was trying not to laugh. I raised my brows at him. "You said I could say anything."

He nodded, barely containing his laugh. "I did."

"Well, that was what I wanted to say." I stepped away from Bourne.

"I see what Cole sees in you," he murmured.

"I'll take that as a compliment. And now I am going to leave you to do whatever it is you're going to do, but can I ask you a favour?"

He chuckled. "Do I have a choice?"

"I'd prefer not. Can you do this somewhere other than near my kitchen table, please?"

His smile finally turned into a laugh. "Only because you used your manners," he said with a wink.

I watched as he hefted Bourne up and led him out the back door. Bourne's neck was a masterpiece of cuts and blood, and I figured King was about to make a huge mess. And that didn't even bother me. I liked the fact he was ridding the Earth of another piece of shit.

"Harlow?" Scarlett's groggy voice floated in from the lounge room and I hurried in there to make sure she was okay.

Kneeling next to her, I said, "How much pain are you in?"

She held her face. "On a scale of one to ten, I'd say a motherfucking eleven. That prick deserves everything he gets. I'm sorry I pretty much passed out, but damn, he hit me hard."

"I slapped him for you."

"You should have fucking punched the cocksucker."

"God no, I didn't want to hurt myself in the process."

She laughed and shook her head at me. "You're a fucking princess, but I do kinda like you."

"Harlow!" Scott came barrelling through the front door at that moment, a look of sheer horror on his face. When he saw me, he stilled, and stared in surprise. "You're okay?"

I stood and wrapped my arms around him.

Home.

He's my home.

His strong arms held me tight and then he ran one hand over my hair. "I'm taking it from the blood on Scarlett's face that Bourne has been here, but where is he now?"

223

"King took him downstairs."

His brow furrowed. "King is here?"

"Yeah, he saved our lives, Scott. If he hadn't turned up when he did, Scarlett and I would be dead by now."

"Fuck." He pressed his lips to my forehead and then pulled his face back to find my gaze. "I think this is the last of all the shit. I think Bourne was the one behind everything."

If I knew my man well, I knew he was itching to get downstairs and help King, so I jerked my head towards the back door. "You should go and see if King needs a hand."

He bent his face so he could whisper in my ear. "You know me too well, sweetheart." When he shifted his face away from mine, his concerned eyes took mine in. "Seriously, though, are you okay?"

I exhaled. "Surprisingly, yes. Don't get me wrong, I'm sick of being threatened by assholes, and I was terrified of him, but I'll be okay."

And I would be.

I had Scott and it looked like this might be the end of all the bad stuff that had been bringing the club down.

We'd stuck together and gotten through it, even when it felt completely overwhelming at times.

We can get through anything so long as we stick together.

Chapter Eighteen
Scott

Two Days Later

It had been two days since we'd taken out Bourne and finally put to rest all the problems Storm had been having. Order had been restored and questions had finally been answered. And I'd told all club members to take a few days and spend them with their families.

It was a sunny January afternoon and I was sitting on my back deck, beer in one hand, my woman in my lap with her tits pressed up against me, and her lips on mine. Order definitely had been restored.

I ran my hand over her ass. "I've missed this," I said when she ended our kiss.

"Missed what?"

"Making out with you, without a fuckin' care in the world. Storm's had so much shit going on for so long now, that I can't remember the last time I could dedicate so many hours to this."

She gave me one of her sexy grins. "I've missed it, too."

A memory flashed in my mind and I chuckled. "Do you remember that three date policy bullshit you tried to pull on me when we first started seeing each other?"

Her grin lit up her face. "I do, and I'll have you know you are the only man I ever broke that policy for."

"Maybe I could bribe you into marriage the same way you tried to bribe me into sex."

"What would this bribe entail?" She tried to plant another kiss on my lips, but I pulled my face away to deny her that kiss.

"I'll give you a kiss if you agree to marry me."

She slapped me playfully on my chest. "Worst marriage proposal *ever*, Scott Cole!"

I laughed. "What? I was only copying the bribe you started us with. I distinctly recall you trying to bribe me with a kiss in exchange for sex."

Leaning in close, she whispered, "I would have done anything to get you to have sex with me back then."

226

I brushed my lips across hers before whispering, "And I would do anything to get you to be my wife now."

She took my hand and placed it on her stomach. Her eyes glistened with tears as she spoke. "Can you feel that?"

"Feel what?" I wasn't sure what she meant. I knew she was referring to our baby, but I couldn't feel it yet.

"Your heart is in here. I get to carry you around with me all day, every day. You might not get to carry my heart, but it's completely yours. Always. I'll marry you and be your wife, but a piece of paper doesn't make any difference to the fact I'm already yours."

Her words meant the fucking world to me.

How the hell did I get so lucky?

"Are you one of those women who wants the full wedding?"

"All I want is you. I don't care how that happens."

That was all I needed. "I'll take care of the wedding."

She was quiet for a moment. "You really are a big softie underneath all that hard exterior, aren't you?"

I kept hold of her gaze. "I'll own that for you. But only for you."

Her face came to mine and she took her time as she kissed me. I could have spent eternity kissing Harlow. Her lips were soft and addicting as they took charge of that kiss, and when her tongue swept across mine, I groaned as my dick grew harder than it already was.

227

I was just about to pick her up and carry her to our bed when a throat cleared and my mum said, "Sorry to interrupt you two, but I brought a casserole over for your dinner. I'm just going to take it inside and put it in your fridge."

After she left us, Harlow's lips curled into a smile while still on mine, and she murmured, "I love your Mum, but this is the worst timing."

Before she could move her face away from mine, I murmured back, "Yeah, but now you don't have to cook that pie you were gonna make for dinner, so I can spend that time fucking you instead."

"That wasn't just any pie I was going to make you. In fact, it wasn't a pie I was making, it was Sex In A Pan."

"What the fuck is Sex In A Pan?"

"It's a cake made with ingredients you can rub all over your body, so I figured we could actually make it together..."

Her eyes glazed over with desire as her voice trailed off and I decided I couldn't wait until later to have her. I needed her now, which meant I had to get rid of my mother.

A minute later, I stood in my kitchen staring at Mum as she rifled through our fridge. "What are you doing?"

Her head popped up so she could look at me. "It's your rubbish day tomorrow so I thought I'd clean out your fridge. Saves you doing it when I know you've got other things you'd rather be doing."

228

Harlow moved behind me and wrapped her arms around my waist. She pressed her face against my back and muffled her soft chuckle.

"Mum, we really appreciate everything you've been doing for us over the last couple of days, but there's no need." She had almost suffocated us with kindness and I couldn't figure out what her actions were all about.

And I really need you to leave now so I can fuck my fiancé.

She waved me away. "I don't mind doing it. I love helping you." Her voice cracked a little when she added, "I can't imagine not being able to do these things for you."

Clarity hit me. "I'm not going anywhere," I said quietly.

Her eyes found mine and I took in the rapid rise and fall of her chest, and her teary eyes. "I know," she whispered, "but everything that's happened just reminded me of how dangerous club life can sometimes be."

Harlow let me go and I knew why. I walked to where Mum stood and embraced her. "I love you," I said. Words I hadn't said to my mother in far too long.

She sobbed quietly in my arms and I knew this wasn't only about her worry for me – this was for all the time we'd lost over the last couple of years. We'd lost each other for a while there, but we'd weathered the storm and come out stronger for it. She wiped her eyes and looked up at me. "I love you, too."

229

I smiled.

Everything's going to be all right.

She closed the fridge, grabbed the bag of rubbish she had, and said, "I'll take this out for you and then I promise I'll leave you guys alone."

Yes.

If I were a praying man, I would have sent a fucking prayer of thanks up to heaven.

Harlow made a strange noise behind me, and when I turned to see what was wrong, she scrunched her face up at me and nodded her head towards Mum.

"What?" I mouthed.

"Ask her to stay for dinner?" she mouthed back.

Fuck.

I bent so I could say quietly, "That's gonna cut into my time with your pussy. You sure you're good with that?"

She smacked me lightly on my chest. "Just ask her, Scott! She obviously wants to spend time with you."

I flattened my lips. "For fuck's sake...the shit I do to keep my women happy," I muttered. Turning back to Mum, I said, "Stay for dinner."

Harlow had been right to insist Mum stayed for dinner. As soon as the words left my mouth, she hit me with the biggest smile I'd seen on her in a long time. "Sounds good," she agreed and then left us to take the rubbish out.

I dragged Harlow to me, pressing her body tight to mine. "I was thinking we should get married on Saturday."

Her jaw dropped open. "That's only four days away!"

"My point exactly. I want to marry you as soon as possible and I figure a Saturday is the best option for everyone to be able to make it."

"We need to lodge a marriage application form or something to get married, Scott. And I think that has to be lodged a month before the wedding."

I grinned. "Good thing I already lodged one."

"What? How? Did you forge my signature?"

"No. I was able to sign it and lodge it, and so long as you sign it before the wedding, we're all good."

Her palms landed on my chest and she attempted to push out of my hold, but I held her tighter so she couldn't.

"Don't fight me, baby. I'm done waiting. I want that ring on your finger," I growled.

She gazed up at me with a smile in her eyes. "I'm not fighting you. I'm just starting to panic, that's all. I need to call Cassie and Madison because I'm going to need help getting a dress, and hair, and shoes, and makeup and all the things a girl needs to be at her best on the day she finally marries the man she loves."

I eased my hold on her, but only a little bit. "I'd marry you without all that shit. I want you clean or dirty, perfectly styled hair or with bedhead, a face full of

231

makeup or straight out of bed in the morning, wedding dress or pyjamas, heels or barefoot, rich or poor." I paused and placed my hand over her heart. "I want *this* with all of that or none of it. You are perfect to me however you come, Harlow."

She stared at me for a long moment. I felt the connection we shared; I always had from the very first moment I laid eyes on her. It was deep, and honest and everything I'd never known I needed or wanted. She finally sorted through her thoughts, and then said, "Now *that's* a proposal worth saying yes to."

I wanted to throw her over my shoulder and carry her caveman-style to our bed.

I wanted to spend hours devouring her body.

I wanted to worship her like the softie she now knew me to be.

Harlow had taken my cold heart and bandaged it with love. She'd shown me how loving someone else could heal your own wounds. And she'd taught me that there really could be a blessing in the storm.

Sometimes the struggle was absolutely worth the outcome.

Chapter Nineteen
Harlow

I blinked my eyes open as my hand landed on Scott's head. I'd been fast asleep, dreaming of his growly voice and his mouth on my body. As it turned out, he *had* been growling words in my ear and his mouth *was* on my body.

Heaven.

I arched my back up off the bed as his tongue flicked over my clit. Fisting his hair, I begged, "Don't ever stop."

He lifted his mouth and his eyes met mine. "Got no plans for that any time soon, sweetheart," he rasped as he scooped his hands under my ass, and lifted my pussy to his mouth. Like I was a feast that he couldn't live without.

God, yes.

Best way to wake up.

I rested my legs over his shoulders and closed my eyes for a moment while he delivered the kind of pleasure only Scott Cole could give. My man's expert mouth and tongue always drove me wild. God had blessed me the day he'd given me this man.

And the best part is I get to have him for the rest of my life.

A shot of bliss ran through my body and I quivered under his touch as he let me go and repositioned me so he could move up the bed. His hands and knees settled on the bed either side of my body, and he bent to kiss my stomach and breasts as he made his way up to my neck and mouth.

"I thought you had no plans to stop what you were doing." I pouted.

His lips caught mine and he bruised them with a rough kiss. "Decided I needed this more," he growled as he ran his cock through my wet folds.

I bit my lip as I lifted my ass off the bed and pressed myself against him. My arms wrapped around his neck, and I let out a low moan. "I'm down with that."

He pushed his cock against my entrance again, still not entering me, but rather, continuing to cause my need for him to increase. "Thought you might be."

234

I tightened my hold on him and dug my fingernails into his skin, loving the hiss that escaped his lips. "You know what I'd be *more* than down with?"

His cock circled my entrance as he asked, "What?"

Good God, he's driving me freaking insane.

I waited for the exact right moment, and when I had it, I wrapped my legs around him and pushed my pussy up to take him inside. "*That,*" I said on a groan as he filled me.

He hissed again. "*Fuck.*" His breathing picked up as he settled himself deep inside. And then he repeated himself. "Fuck."

I rocked my hips, trying to get him to fuck me, but he seemed content just to be inside me while I rocked back and forth. "Scott..."

He dipped his mouth to mine and kissed me before saying, "Yeah?"

I exhaled a frustrated breath. "Are you going to fuck me or are you just going to let your dick fall asleep inside me?"

He pulled his face away from mine and a sexy grin spread across his lips. "I fuckin' love it when you talk dirty to me, baby."

I raised my brows. "Well?"

He pulled his cock out and slowly entered me again, going as deep as he could before rocking inside me for a moment. "So fuckin' demanding," he muttered.

235

His slow moves were excruciatingly pleasurable. I loved the change to his usual pace, but I craved his hard and fast ways.

I need him to fuck me.

And make me come.

He held himself over me, hands planted either side of my body, and continued his slow and deep torture. His eyes glazed over with satisfaction and every now and then, he grunted as he tried to delay his orgasm.

"That feel good, baby?" he asked as he began to pick up the pace.

My core clenched as I tried to focus. *It feels so damn good, I can hardly concentrate.* "Yes," I panted.

He lowered his body a little and I clung to him as he began thrusting harder and faster.

Yes.

Oh God, yes.

Bliss overtook my mind and body, and I focused all my attention on Scott and the orgasm he was giving me.

So close.

Oh, fuck.

I rocked harder with him.

Nearly there.

Please.

Now.

I gripped him tighter, trying desperately to get the orgasm to shatter through my body.

Come on.

"Fuck!" he roared as he came.

I rocked harder again.

Frantic.

Please.

I need it now.

"Scott...oh God, yes!" I screamed out as I orgasmed.

Finally.

My toes curled and I kept clinging to Scott as my release lit every one of my nerve endings. *So damn good.*

We held each other while we came down from the high, catching our breaths and riding out the waves of pleasures.

When Scott collapsed onto the bed beside me, he rested his hand on my stomach, and said, "Morning, sweetheart."

I softly laughed while rolling onto my side and snuggling against him. As I rested my head on his shoulder, he placed his arm around me to hold me close.

I loved this time with him. That feeling of being joined, and the connection of our souls, centred me and reminded me of how loved I was. It reminded me I had so many things to be thankful for. It also reminded me I wasn't in my struggle alone.

"I'm scared," I whispered, finally giving voice to my fear.

He turned his face and watched me silently for a moment. "Of losing the baby?"

I swallowed back the tears that threatened. I'd done enough crying over the past few months, I didn't want to cry any more. "Yes."

He shifted so he was facing me, our bodies chest-to-chest. Running his fingers through my hair, he said, "I know. But we're going to do this together, Harlow. You're going to keep talking to me about that fear, and I'm going to be here for you every step of the way. And no matter what happens, we'll face it, and deal with it. *Together.*"

His eyes searched mine, probably seeking some kind of acknowledgement that I would do this with him, and not shut him out again. I needed to give him that. I needed him to know I would never shut him out ever again.

I nodded, and then I gave him something I should have given him months ago. "Will you come with me to my next appointment with Jane? I want to talk this out with her and I think it would be good for both of us to be involved in that conversation." I'd never asked him to attend any of my psychology appointments because I'd always felt like it was my problem and so I should deal with it myself. But I'd come a long way, and now I realised that my problems were Scott's problems, too.

"I'll be there," he replied, and even though he'd only said three words, I knew those three words had deep meaning for him.

Leaning into him, I brushed a kiss across his lips. "Thank you."

Hope soared in my heart. I was scared, but Scott helped empower me to believe I could get through this. *We* would get through this.

"Call me when you're ready to be picked up," Scott said after I kissed him goodbye later that morning. I had a hair appointment scheduled and he'd insisted on bringing me. Since the incidents with Rogue and Bourne, he'd hardly let me out of his sight and I figured that making sure I got to my appointment safely was just another way for him to feel reassured of my safety. I would give him that; I'd give him whatever he needed because he gave me so much.

"I will, but won't you be busy with the club today?"

"Only this morning. By the time you finish here, I'll have time."

"Okay, baby, I'll see you then."

He jerked his chin at Roxie's shop, letting me know he'd wait for me to go inside. With one last kiss, I left him, loving the fact his eyes were on me as I walked away. Scott made me feel ten times the woman I was just by the way he loved me.

"Morning, beautiful," Bobby greeted me as I pushed through the front door of the salon.

I loved Bobby, one of Roxie's hairdressers. His sarcastic and over-the-top behaviour always made me smile. "Hey, Bobby. How's your morning going?"

He rolled his eyes and gave me a flick of his wrist. "Don't even go there, Harlow. I woke up this morning ready to take on the world and then the world took me on instead. I met the man of my dreams last night, took him home and showed him all the ways I could make *his* dreams come true, and then this morning, his ex messaged him to say he wanted him back. He sat in *my* bed and had a heart-to-fucking-heart with his ex and then promptly told me he had a great time with me, but he had to skip breakfast because he was now having it with his ex." His eyes widened and he placed his hand on his hip. Waving his other hand in the air, he continued, "So, *I* promptly replied and told him to get the fuck out of my bed so I could torch my sheets, along with my memories of him."

Poor Bobby. He always fell fast and hard, and I couldn't keep track of the number of times he'd had his heart broken. "Better to find out now that he's an ass, rather than down the track when you're committed to him, right?"

He pursed his lips together as if he really wasn't convinced. "I know you're right, but hot damn, this guy had *it*. And it's not often that comes along."

"I hear you, Bobby, and I totally get it. I met a lot of guys with *it*, and in the end, *it* turned out to be a false

240

promise. Keep looking; eventually the right man will sweep you off your feet."

"Pfft, it's easy enough for you to say that when you've got the Coleminator warming your fucking bed. Just for the record, I would take that man any which way he comes." He waved me away. "Roxie's in the back room. You should go because I don't want to look at that happy face of yours today." And with that, he looked back down at the paperwork he was filling out, and proceeded to block me out.

I laughed. Leaning across the counter, I whispered, "FYI, I'm marrying the Coleminator. I'll be sure to send you an invitation so you can drool."

His eyes snapped to mine. Pointing to the back room where Roxie was, he bossed me. "Go! If I hear one more word about Scott Cole, I can not be held accountable for my actions."

Roxie appeared in the doorway of the back room. Narrowing her eyes on Bobby, she said, "Is he whinging about that douche from last night again?"

"Yeah. Poor Bobby," I replied as I walked past her into the small room.

"Poor Bobby?" She turned to face me and watched as I stored my handbag in a safe place. Crossing her arms over her chest, she said, "That man throws his heart at guys. He needs to get over that shit and start being more selective."

I shook my head at her. "You and your cold heart, Roxie."

"No, me and my *practical* heart. He's worse than a schoolgirl with a new crush every day. I swear, I'm going to lock him up for a couple of months and teach him some new ways." She came to me and reached for my hair. "What are we doing today? You only just had it coloured."

A huge smile made its way across my face. "I'm getting married," I announced, a little breathless with excitement.

In typical Roxie form, she didn't even bat an eyelid. "It's about time."

"Yeah, it really is."

She let my hair go and started rummaging through a cupboard. "So this is why you've got all the girls coming in today. I was wondering."

I'd asked Madison, Velvet and Layla to come today so I could get their opinion on my hair for the wedding. But that wasn't my real reason. After everything that had happened with the club recently, I figured we needed some girl time. The club had to rebuild, and I truly believed that involved their women. We had to be strong so they could, too. Men would never fully grasp this, but girl time was more than just talking girl stuff and hanging out. It was soul time.

"Oh, my God!" Madison screamed from behind me. "Did I just hear that right? You and Scott are getting married?"

I turned with a grin. "Yes!"

It was like her whole body was lit up. Her happiness shone from her. She wrapped her arms around me and hugged me tight. "I am *so* happy for you both!"

She held me for a long time, and when she finally let me go, I said softly, "Thank you. And thank you for coming today. I'm excited, but I'm also nervous. I need my girls around this week."

"I'm here for you, honey. Whatever you need. And - " she stepped aside, " – I brought Sophia with me. I figured it was time for her initiation."

I welcomed Sophia with a smile. "We're throwing you in the deep end today. Sorry about that."

She returned my smile. "Congratulations on your engagement. And I love being thrown in the deep end."

I hardly knew Sophia, but it was easy to pick up on her warmth and friendliness. "You're going to fit right in with us girls. Griff's not going to know what hit him."

"We might need to ease him into it. I do love him, but he's taken a while to get his shit together with regards to introducing me to the club," Sophia said.

Velvet arrived at that point and threw her two cents in. "I think you've got the patience of a saint."

"I've got all the patience in the world for that man. I've never known a man to be so good to me," Sophia replied, and I loved her a little more for saying that.

"I think Griff's an amazing man, too," I said. "And I'm so glad he's found a woman as good as you to love him."

243

Roxie interrupted us. "Oh, God, enough of the love fest. I may gag soon. Let's start thinking about your hair for the wedding."

We headed out to the front of the shop and as I took a seat, Bobby said, "Layla just rang. She can't make it today. Something about Blade, and him having the day off, and her knowing you girls would totally understand."

Velvet took the seat next to me. "After two full days of Nash loving, I totally understand where that girl's coming from."

Bobby sighed. "I knew I should just have called in sick. Listening to your sexcapades with those Storm men may just kill me today."

We all broke out into laughter, and happiness bubbled through me. This was what made life good – friends and family who loved you, and who shared the good and bad with you. Friends and family who held your hand and guided you when you couldn't guide yourself. I knew I still had work to do on myself, and that the journey would never be clear of hardships, but with these girls by my side, the bumps would be a little easier to navigate.

Chapter Twenty
Scott

"Where are we at with Julio's guys?" I asked Nash during Church that morning. After King and I had dealt with Bourne the other day, we'd pulled everyone together and delivered a warning to Julio's crew to leave town – the kind of warning that involved blood and not many men left standing.

"The few that were left standing have all headed back to Adelaide."

I expelled the breath I hadn't realised I was holding.

Thank fuck.

I nodded as I relaxed back into my chair. "And King has advised me that he's promised hell to Adelaide Storm if they retaliate." I looked around the room, taking in the serious expressions the guys all wore. Leaning forward again, I rested my elbows on the table and said, "This is all over. Finally. Now we rebuild our club and hope to fuck that we can have some peace for a long time."

I watched as their serious expressions gave way to smiles and nods of relief. And all I could think was that it was about time.

Griff took over to discuss some pressing matters involving Trilogy and Indigo, and once they were all sorted, I spoke up again. "This Saturday, I'm getting married - " Wolf whistles and cheers cut me off, and I gave them that for a moment before taking control again. "If you're in town this weekend, I want you at the wedding."

"Wouldn't miss it for the fucking world," J said as he grinned at me. "Never actually thought I'd see the day that Scott Cole got married."

"Smartass," I muttered before calling an end to Church.

As everyone filed out of the room, I called Griff aside. "I want you to be my best man."

He listened to my request, his expression not changing. However, his breathing picked up, and then he replied, "Means a lot to me, Scott. After everything we've been through over the past few months, it means a fucking lot."

"I didn't handle shit very well when you told me about your family, and I'm sorry, brother. You need to know that you are more family to me than some of my own blood family. I'd be honoured to have you by my side when I marry Harlow." There wasn't much I regretted in my life, but I wasn't proud of the way I'd reacted when Griff shared his past with me.

He straightened and pushed his shoulders back as he said, "I'd be honoured to be your best man."

I grinned. A load had been lifted off my shoulders now that we'd had that conversation. Slapping him on the back, I made a suggestion. "We need a beer."

He returned my grin and nodded his agreement. "Or two."

Some people didn't understand the brotherhood of Storm. It was, however, what I believed in the most in my life. To trust and believe in something so much that you would lay down your life for it – that was what the brotherhood was to me.

It was family.

"Harlow tells me that you're the one planning the wedding. So weird," Cassie said to me that afternoon. I'd picked Harlow up from the hairdresser and planned a long afternoon in bed with her, but her best friend had arrived just as Harlow had run her tongue along my cock.

Worst fucking timing.

"Why is that weird?" I asked while grabbing a beer from the fridge.

"Well, firstly it's just strange for the man to do the planning, but add to that fact you're a biker...never saw that one coming, dude."

Harlow laughed the nervous laugh she'd adopted when she was around Cassie and me. Her friend never hesitated to challenge me, and Harlow seemed hesitant about that. She needn't have been. While I may not have always agreed with everything Cassie said, I respected the hell out of her honesty.

I took a swig of beer and sat at the table on the back deck with them. "So bikers can't organise shit for their women?"

Cassie drank some of the wine I'd just poured her. "You've gotta admit it's strange. When I think of bikers, I think of men who do manly things while their women run around after them."

I raised my brows. "When the fuck do you see Harlow running around after me?"

Cassie laughed and nodded. "True. She doesn't. The fact remains, though, that I think it's weird for a club president to be taking charge of a wedding."

I drank some more beer as I contemplated what she'd said. "I'll concede that it's not the norm, but I'm not about the norm. From the very beginning, I knew I'd make Harlow my wife. Watching her go through what she has over the last few months has been hard, but as dark as some of those days were, they only reinforced to me how much I loved her. She gives me so much, the least I can do is give her a wedding she'll always remember."

Cassie stared at me like I had two heads. She then turned to Harlow and said, "Jeez, I need me a Scott Cole. You are one lucky bitch."

Harlow's eyes had misted over, but she smiled as she said, "I know. And I can help you find your Mr Perfect. I have lots of ideas of where we could look."

Cassie rolled her eyes. "Please, I've searched high and low. There aren't any good men out there who aren't already taken."

Harlow shook her head. "I don't believe that. I'll find you one."

"Okay, girl, you find me a man while I find you an art gallery to show your paintings. Where are you at with those paintings I saw in your art room?"

"They're finished," Harlow replied, and for the first time in a long time, I didn't hear any fear in her voice. Her standard response when it came to her art over the last six months had been a reluctance to even consider pursuing an art exhibition.

Excitement flared on Cassie's face. "Awesome! And you still want to do this?"

249

Harlow took a deep breath and then nodded. "Yes. I'm scared, but if it doesn't make you sweat, it's not worth doing, right?"

Cassie burst into laughter. "Well, fuck me, you *do* listen to me!" Cassie had been saying those exact words to Harlow for a long time now, and Harlow had done her best to ignore her. I was fucking ecstatic to hear her change of heart.

Harlow grinned. "Sign me up before I change my mind."

"Oh no, girl, you never get to change your mind now. This is happening!"

"Harlow!" Scarlett's voice sounded from the front door.

"Shit," Harlow muttered as she stood. "She's probably been knocking on the door and we couldn't hear her."

I groaned as she left us. Scarlett had a way of irritating the fuck out of me, and I thought we had tied up all our loose ends with her, and sent her on her way.

"What's wrong?" Cassie asked. "Don't you like her?"

"I don't dislike her, but she has the ability to frustrate me in a matter of seconds."

Cassie scoffed. "Doesn't everyone have that ability with you?"

"I'll admit I have a temper, but I've been working on it. Scarlett messes with my concentration where that's concerned."

The back door opened and Scarlett appeared. "Oh hey, there's the resident moody biker."

I stood. "And to what do we owe this pleasure?" I asked, not even attempting to hide my sarcasm.

"I left a pair of my shoes here. And I also wanted to say thank you to you."

"Really?"

She huffed out a breath. "Yes, *really*. Don't be a prick, Scott. I'm trying to do the right thing here. As much as you and I have had run-ins and said cross words to each other, you came through for me when most don't, and I appreciate what you did. So, thank you."

Scarlett was unlike most women I'd met in my life. She said it like it was, didn't put up with bullshit, and as far as I could work out, she had balls the size of most men's. "I appreciate that, but let's get one thing straight – you kicking me in the balls is *not* classified as a run-in in my book, it's a lot worse than a run-in, and it won't ever happen again."

A grin teased her lips, but didn't quite form. "It will if you act like an ass."

"Jesus," I muttered with a shake of my head. Eyeing Harlow, I said, "I'm gonna leave you girls to it, but don't take too long, baby. We've got shit to do, if you recall."

Harlow tried not to laugh. "I do."

I left her to her laughing about my situation of an unresolved hard-on, and headed into the lounge room. I'd just settled in front of the television and put my feet up

251

when Lisa came through the front door. We'd given her a key a while ago, but she didn't use it very often, so I was surprised to see her.

"Hi, Scott," she greeted me.

"Hi, darlin', how's your day been?" I motioned for her to take a seat. As far as she'd come with her confidence over the last year, she still had a way to go. Feeling comfortable enough to make herself at home in ours was something Harlow and I had been encouraging, yet she was still a little shy about it.

She settled on the edge of the couch. "I qualified to compete in the school swimming carnival which is on next week, so it was a good day today."

"What day is it on next week?"

"Friday. Why?"

"Can I come and watch?"

Her body stilled as she stared at me. "Really?"

I fought to hold my cool. It still killed me when she displayed surprise at Harlow's or my interest in her life. "Yes, really."

A smile slowly filled her face. "Sure, that would be awesome. Do you think Harlow can come, too?"

"If she can get the time off work, I'm sure she'll come." Harlow would do everything in her power to be at that swimming carnival. Of that, I was sure. "Is your mum going?"

She nodded. "Yes. So, I'll have you and her there, and maybe Harlow." Her excited voice hit me in the gut. Hard and swift. It was so easy to make a child happy, and yet some parents failed at it. Harlow and I wouldn't. We would make sure our child knew deep in their soul how loved they were. And we would continue to find ways to show Lisa how much we cared about her.

"Harlow spoke to you about Saturday?"

"Yes! We're going dress shopping tomorrow after school. I can't wait – it'll be my first real dress." She suddenly reached into her pocket and pulled something out. Handing it to me, she said, "I nearly forgot, I have your money to give back to you."

Frowning, I asked, "What money?"

She shoved it at me. "The money you lent me for my sport uniform."

I held my hand up to indicate I didn't want it. "You keep it. Either give it back to your mum or keep it for emergencies." I hoped she would choose to keep it – knowing she had cash on hand put my mind at ease.

Her eyes held mine, and they softened as she nodded and put the money away. "Thank you." Her voice was quiet, but full of emotion, and I knew my gesture meant a lot to her.

I also knew she would be uncomfortable with this, so I changed the subject. Jerking my chin at the television, I said, "You wanna watch The Simpsons?"

She grinned and finally kicked back on the couch. "Yeah."

Lisa loved The Simpsons. Me, not so much, but watching it had become our thing. It zoned her into her happy place, and I would do anything to give her that happy place, so, The Simpsons, it was.

Harlow stood in front of the mirror in our bathroom, in her sexy, red lingerie, smoothing moisturiser onto her face. She was completely engrossed in what she was doing, so she didn't notice me standing in the doorway. I took the opportunity to appreciate her beauty. Harlow was easily the most beautiful woman I'd ever laid eyes on, and as I trailed my gaze over her curves, I grew hard just like I always did. She never failed to turn me on, and I knew I was the luckiest bastard in the world for the simple fact I'd now have her by my side for the rest of my life.

"Are you checking out my ass?" Her voice jolted me from my thoughts.

Finding her eyes, I smiled and moved to stand behind her. Placing my hands on her ass, I murmured, "No, but I was getting there." I bent and kissed her neck, letting my lips linger on her skin for a few moments.

"I'm sorry Cassie ended up staying for so long." Cassie stayed for dinner and hadn't gone home until just after nine, but I hadn't cared because it made Harlow happy to have her there. And, fuck, seeing Harlow as happy as she'd been over the last couple of days made *me* happy.

My lips skimmed over her skin along her shoulders as I said, "I didn't mind, but just so you know, I'm as hard for you now as I was when she first arrived." My hands slid around her waist to land on her stomach as I ground my dick against her ass. "Jesus, I'm not sure who the fuck I'm kidding, sweetheart, I'm always this hard for you."

She turned in my hold and looped her hands around my neck. Her lips found mine and she kissed me with the kind of passion that had the power to steal a man's breath. I knew it did because she stole mine all the time. When she ended the kiss, she said, "That day you brought Monty into the vet surgery, I never imagined in my wildest dreams that we'd end up here."

"I thought you were so judgemental then. Fuck, was I wrong." The memories flooded my mind, and I cringed at the thought I could have lost my chance with her because of my wrong first impressions.

"Thank goodness Madison invited me to that barbecue." Her fingers threaded through my hair and she pulled my face to hers again for another kiss.

I lost myself in that kiss.

I lost myself in Harlow.

My hands cupped her ass as my tongue tangled with hers. I lifted her and she wrapped her legs around me, holding tight while I turned us and backed her up against the wall.

"Fuck, baby, you do know that you own me, don't you?" I rasped as I drowned in her.

Her gaze met mine. "No, it's the other way around, Scott. I'm completely yours, body and soul. Always."

I held her up, pressing my body hard against hers, my mouth devouring her in my desperate need to consume her – to consume everything she offered, and more. I was so fucking greedy for her.

"I need you now," I growled. "I can't wait any longer." Taking a step back, I placed her down, and frantically undid my jeans to free my cock. At the same time, she slid her panties down, and then I lifted her top over her head. When I finally had her standing naked in front of me, my hands went to her breasts right before my mouth did.

"Just a quick taste..." I promised in between licking and sucking her nipples. "Fuck, you taste so good."

"Scott..." she moaned my name as she climbed into my hold again.

She needs me as much as I need her.

I didn't wait until I had a firm hold of her – I couldn't. Instead, I thrust inside, my eyes rolling shut as I groaned at how fucking good her pussy felt pulsing around my dick.

She clung to me as I fucked her.

Finally.

I'd been thinking about this moment all day, and while I knew once tonight wouldn't even begin to satisfy my need for her, this was a damn good start.

256

We chased our release as hard and as fast as we could, and it didn't take long. Pleasure exploded through my body as we came together. It touched every part of me, both physical and mental.

This part of sex with Harlow was what I had been missing all my life. I'd had a lot of sex before finding her, and none of it had ever come close to touching me in the way it did with Harlow.

Harlow joined all the pieces of my soul together.

She made me whole.

Chapter Twenty-One
Harlow

All my life I dreamt of the day I would walk down the aisle and tell the man I loved that I would spend the rest of my life with him. I was a romantic from way back. But I never imagined it would be like this. Never did I imagine the love I found would be what Scott and I had.

Magic.

That was the only word I could use to describe it that would do our love justice.

The day of our wedding had arrived and I was in full preparation mode. Roxie had done my hair, and Velvet had made my face look more beautiful than I'd ever seen it.

Cassie smiled at me. She was my only bridesmaid and looked beautiful with her long hair up and her face also done beautifully. We'd chosen a long, strapless, red dress for her and the colour was perfect against her tanned skin. "Babe, we got ready in record time. Scott would be impressed that you're ready early."

My mum laughed as she joined us. Roxie and Velvet had just worked their magic on her, too. She took hold of my hand and squeezed it. "You look beautiful, Harlow."

Catching sight of myself in the full-length mirror, I had to agree with her – I *felt* beautiful. With Madison and Cassie's help, I'd chosen a strapless organza gown with a fitted bodice of ruches and a cascading skirt of ruffles that flowed to the ground. Silver glittered in the narrow band of embroidery at the waist. While the dress was beautifully elegant, I'd still managed to add my country style to the outfit with my turquoise boots. We'd left my hair down in soft curls and Roxie had swept the front part of it back and secured it with my mother's silver clip that she'd worn at her wedding.

Madison swept into the room, her hands full with things I couldn't quite make out. Smiling as she came to me, she said, "So, you've got the something old, but you still need new, borrowed and blue."

Touching my necklace, I curled my finger along the chain. "Scott gave me this the other day, so it's my new."

259

Madison narrowed her eyes on the necklace. "Oh my goodness, that is beautiful." She looked back up at my face. "My brother has surprised the hell out of me this week. Who knew he could be so deep?"

Scott had the necklace designed with a swirly S and H that were connected in the middle with a lightning strike. My heart beat with happiness just thinking about the thought he'd put into it. "I didn't know the symbolism of lightning until he told me. Apparently the Celts believe that wherever lightning strikes, it is a spot of the sacred and holy, and signifies a connection with infinite power. The Chinese associate lightning with fertility – it's a blessing that leads to nourishing rains and new life."

"I knew that man was good from the moment I met him when he brought me a fridge," Mum said softly, her eyes misting with tears. "It's because of him that I know I can go away and leave you in good hands."

Madison's eyes had brimmed over with tears, too. "Shit, now he's making me cry and it's going to ruin my makeup."

Velvet handed tissues out. "I'll be having words with that man for making you all cry and wrecking my makeup job."

Laughing, I said, "I feel like I should be the one crying, and yet, I'm the only one here without tears in my eyes." I glanced at Roxie and winked. "Well, besides our resident non-crying, practical ballbreaker over here."

She raised her brows back at me. "What can I say...me and romance have a long, hard relationship, and it takes a lot to crack through my heart."

"Wait!" exclaimed Madison. "Did you say you're going away?" she asked Mum.

"Yes, after the fire at the café, I've decided to travel for a few months. I've wanted to visit Italy for as long as I can remember, and I'm not getting any younger, so now's as good a time as any. And with Harlow wanting to pursue her art, and our lease on the café almost up, it feels like the universe is speaking to me and telling me to go." Her eyes lit up as she added, "I leave at the end of next week. But I'll be back in time for the birth of my grandchild."

"You better be!" I said, not being able to imagine getting through that without her.

"So, tell me, how are you getting to the church?" Roxie asked as she packed up her stuff.

"Oh, she's not getting married in a church," Madison said with a sly smile.

At Roxie's enquiring look, I said, "I don't know where I'm getting married. Scott kept that from me, but I do know that King is driving me there. He'll be here soon to pick up me and Cassie."

"King?" Velvet asked, clearly confused.

"Yeah, Scott asked him to stay for the wedding. They've got this whole bonding thing happening after King saved my life. I mean, it's not like the bonding thing that girls experience, but I think it's safe to say that for

261

the rest of his life, if King asks Scott for help, it will be given, no questions asked. And I think that asking King to be involved in the wedding was Scott's way of expressing what King's actions meant to him." I paused for a moment before adding, "Or I could be reading far too much into male thinking and none of that is true. Really, who knows what our men are thinking..."

Madison agreed with me. "Too true, but like I said, Scott has blown me away this week while we've been arranging this wedding. I've seen a side to him that I've never seen."

"You and Scott organised the wedding?" Roxie said.

"He did most of it and just asked for my help on a few things," Madison replied. "I think Wilder did a lot of running around for him, getting stuff for the reception sorted out."

"King's here," Velvet announced, peering through the curtains in my lounge room.

Butterflies fluttered in my tummy. Not nervous butterflies, though. These were of the excited kind – the butterflies you felt when you couldn't wait for something to happen.

A few moments later, King's boots sounded on the front steps and then he knocked on the door. Cassie opened it and greeted him, and I didn't miss the way his eyes lazily checked out her body. "Well, hello there," he murmured.

Cassie shook her head. "You bikers just don't give a fuck about subtlety, do you?"

He grinned and it had to be said, King had sexy covered. It wasn't just the muscles he barely hid underneath jeans and a fitted black tee that screamed 'hot biker dude' that qualified him as sexy in my mind; it was more about the ease and confidence with which he moved, and the attitude he projected that even if shit was going down, he had it covered. And the effortless way he moved between the different emotions he felt – nothing seemed too hard for King. "Subtlety doesn't warm a bed at night," he said as he entered the house.

"It sure doesn't," Cassie agreed as she shut the door and followed him.

King's gaze met mine and although he was a hard man, I saw some soft in him today. "Scott Cole is a lucky bastard," he said, his eyes remaining steady on mine. I had to give him credit – he didn't lower his gaze once. The man clearly had respect for his brother.

"Thank you," I said with a smile.

He nodded once. "You ready, beautiful?"

"Almost," Madison cut in. "We just have to finish taking care of her borrowed and her blue."

King hit her with a frown. "Her borrowed and her blue? What the fuck is that?"

"He speaks my language," Roxie said with her signature sarcasm.

"Wedding traditions," Mum advised him and then said to Madison, "I took care of her something blue last night."

This was news to me. "What is it?"

"I stitched the date of your first date with Scott and today's date into your wedding dress. In blue."

My eyes widened in surprise. "How did you know the date of our first date?"

"I asked him." She watched me with the look of a proud mother – the kind of look that said, *'You did so well, he even remembers dates'*, because to my mother, remembering the special moments meant everything to her.

Madison's face resembled the way I felt. She stared at my mother in utter surprise. Turning to me, she muttered, "J has a lot to learn from my brother. Okay, so we have blue covered, and I have these if you want, for the borrowed."

She passed me a beautiful pair of earrings. "Are these yours?" I asked.

"Yes. I wore them when I married J, so they have some meaning. We could hand them down to our daughters when they get married - God willing we have daughters - and start a Cole/Reilly family tradition if you want."

Family tradition.

Love rushed through me and I threw my arms around her. "I love you, Madison Reilly. I would love to start that tradition with you." When I let her go, I reached for a tissue because tears finally threatened to ruin my makeup.

Madison smiled at me through her own tears. "Quick, King, you need to get her out of here before we all become blubbering messes."

"I couldn't agree more," he said. "Nothing worse than crying females."

As I scooped my dress up and walked downstairs to the car – Scott's Charger – my heart was full to almost bursting levels.

We'd all made it through the storm and now I got to live my happy ever after.

Chapter Twenty-Two
Scott

"I do."

Harlow beamed up at me as I said the words I never thought would come out of my mouth. She stood in front of me, in all her beauty, and I was sure my heart would explode out of my chest. I thought I'd felt everything I'd ever feel for her already, but I was wrong. In that moment, I knew this truly was just the beginning of a whole new range of emotions. And as much as I was a man who'd gotten through life up until Harlow without feeling or expressing love, I was fucking down with feeling all of this. *As long as she is by my side.*

I hardly heard the words the celebrant said after I said my vows, but I sure as fuck heard her say, "You may now kiss the bride."

Pressing my lips to Harlow's, I growled, "Mrs Cole." She then showed me how much she loved those words on my lips with the kind of kiss that should be made illegal. When she finally let me go, I said, "Fuck, baby, you do know I have to walk out of here in front of everyone we know, right?"

She hit me with that sexy grin of hers and nodded. "Yes."

Shaking my head at her, I returned her grin and muttered, "Thanks to that kiss, I'll be doing it with a raging hard-on."

"Nothing you've never done before," she threw back.

She had a point.

The celebrant distracted me from my thoughts and moved us to sit down and sign the wedding certificates before finally announcing us as Mr and Mrs Cole.

Taking hold of my wife's hand, I walked us down the aisle, which was a long stretch of red carpet the boys had sourced for me.

Harlow leaned in and said, "You picked the exact right spot for our wedding. I'll never forget the first time you brought me here, and now I'll never forget it as the place you made all my dreams come true."

Fuck.

I figured the park at Wynnum that I'd brought her on our first date was a great location to exchange our vows, but I hadn't factored in how much it would mean to her.

"I hope I can make all your dreams come true, sweetheart." *I'm gonna work my ass off to make that happen.*

She tightened her grip on my hand. "You already have, Scott. I'm living my dream."

Like a fucking drug straight to my veins.

And like the junkie I was, I craved every high Harlow could give me, and I would do whatever the fuck it took to ensure I got that high every day for the rest of my life.

When we made it to the end of the red carpet, I stopped her and took her in my arms. "I love you, Harlow Cole." I placed my hand on her belly. "And the fact you're going to be the mother to my child makes me the happiest man on this planet. *I'm* the one living my dream."

A dream I never knew I had.

A dream I'd go to the ends of the earth to protect.

Her beautiful green eyes searched mine, whispering a million promises, and then finally they twinkled with mischief, and she said, "Scott Cole does sweet really, really, *really* good. Who would have known?"

"That secret stays with us," I bossed her.

"And there's the man I love, all bossy and shit."

The man I love.

I'd never get tired of hearing her say that.

Brushing my lips across hers, I said, "Okay, Mrs Cole, we have a reception to get through, and then I'm going to take you home and bless your body with my mouth and my tongue."

"And your cock?"

I chuckled. "Fuck, woman, that dirty mouth..." I moved my mouth to her ear. "Always with my cock. I've been waving that thing around like freaking King Shit since the day I met you."

I'd repeated the words she'd said to me the night she first set foot in Indigo, and I wondered if she would remember. When her mouth fell open and she gasped, I knew she had.

"You remembered that all this time?" she asked, clearly stunned.

"There's nothing about you, baby, that I don't remember."

And there wasn't.

Harlow James had stumbled into my life and turned it upside down, and I'd remember every step of our journey. I might have been the one who'd taken command of our relationship, and bossed her into being with me, but she'd taken command of my heart and would always own it.

Epilogue
Harlow

One Year Later

"Sit with Uncle Blade while I go and see where Daddy is," I said to Aurora as I made my way to where Blade sat with Layla.

His eyes lit up when he saw us approaching, and his arms automatically stretched out to take my daughter from me.

"Thanks," I said. "I just want to go and find Scott, and then I promise I'll be back for her."

Layla grinned. "Don't rush, Harlow. Honestly, he can't get enough of her."

I watched as Blade blew raspberries on Aurora's belly, and decided Layla wasn't lying. "Looks like babies might be in your future?"

Blade diverted his attention from Aurora for a moment and said, "Yes, they are, but my wife seems to think we should wait a little while longer before we start trying."

Layla sighed, but I could tell she wanted this as much as he did. "All I said was that I wanted another six months or so to get my bar operating at more of a profit, and then we could start working on a baby."

"It's a good thing I'm a patient man," he muttered before going back to playing with Aurora.

"It'll happen," Layla mouthed and I nodded in agreement before leaving them to go and find Scott. I knew it would happen for them because Blade was a man who made sure he got what he wanted. And as much as Layla was a kickass chick who pulled him into line when needed, we all knew she needed Blade as much as she needed the air she breathed. They were a couple you just knew would last forever.

"Harlow!" Velvet called out from the table where she sat with Nash.

Changing my direction, I headed over to see what she wanted. "What's up?"

"I just wanted to tell you that Scarlett's done an amazing job!"

Looking around at the decorations in the restaurant, I agreed. Scarlett had brought Trilogy to life. "She really has."

"She might be a moody bitch, but she's pulled off a great party today," Nash admitted with only a small amount of grumbling in his tone. It was no secret that he and Scarlett clashed, but he always gave credit where it was due. "Fuck knows how Wilder manages to work with her as closely as he does and not kill her, though."

At my suggestion, Wilder had hired Scarlett just after Scott and I got married. I decided Storm's restaurants could do with an image update, and after seeing examples of Scarlett's decorating talents, I knew she was the right person for the job. She hadn't wanted to work for Storm, but her dwindling finances had dictated a need to find work, and the universe had conspired to bring us all together.

The rest was history.

Well, maybe not. Maybe there was more to this story. I watched as Scarlett argued with Wilder over something and wondered how long it would take those two to admit their attraction. They'd known each other a year now, and the sparks were wild.

"Have you seen Scott?" I asked Nash.

"No, but check with Griff. He's with Sophia at the bar," he suggested.

"Thanks, will do," I said.

A few moments later, I met Sophia's gaze and smiled. Griff sat facing the bar and Sophia stood in front of him with her arms around his neck. I'd known her for a year now, and I swore she seemed happier every passing week. The same could be said for Griff. He'd gone from a man of few words, who I hardly knew, to one of my closest friends over this past year. "Hey, Harlow," she greeted me. "Great party."

"It would be if I could find my husband," I grumbled.

Griff turned his head. "I saw him about ten minutes ago, out in the kitchen. Try there, otherwise ask Wilder."

My impatience was kicking in.

I need to do this now.

"Okay, thanks. Oh, and your housewarming is next weekend, right?" They'd recently built a new home and had finally moved in.

Sophia beamed. "Yes, you guys are coming, aren't you? For the love of God, *please* tell me you are. I've got so many people coming who I don't even really know, partners of work mates and friends of my sisters, and you just know I'm going to spend all day rambling about shit if I get nervous. I need you to be there, Harlow, to help centre me and tell me to calm down." Her eyes bulged with desperation and I couldn't stop myself from laughing. Sophia was uniquely her own woman and it was one of the many things I loved about her. The way words just fell out of her mouth always made me smile.

273

Especially that. There should be more women like her –
we could all do with the honesty.

I reached out and placed my hand on her arm. "I promise I'll be there."

She exhaled her relief. "Oh, thank goodness."

"I'll be back soon, but I really need to find Scott."

She waved me away. "Go."

A couple of moments later, I pushed through the door that led to the kitchen. It was a hive of activity, but Scott was not out there.

Damn.

Where is he?

I pulled out my phone and sent him another text, my third so far.

Me: Where are you???? Stop ignoring me or else I will withdraw husband privileges for at least a week.

His reply came through swiftly. Funny how threats like that always worked with men.

Scott: I could go a week, but you couldn't.

Me: Ha! You wanna test that theory?

Scott: Sure. I give you two days at the most before you come begging for my cock.

Me: Tell me where you are and I will come begging for it now.

Scott: I'm in the car park.

Me: Are you hiding from me?

Scott: Fuck no.

Me: Lucky.

When I finally caught sight of him, my heart swelled with love. My hand absently moved to my stomach as I stilled and watched him.

He was with Lisa and they both had their heads under the hood of his Charger. She was listening to him intently while he pointed at various parts of the engine and explained something to her. Memories of my own father doing the same thing slammed into me, and tears pricked my eyes.

I walked the short distance to them, and they both turned their heads when they heard me approaching.

"Hey, Harlow," Lisa said with an easy smile.

"Hi, Honey," I returned her smile before looking at Scott. "Hey." *God, I love this man. Hard.*

He leant over and kissed me. "Sorry, sweetheart, Lisa's assignment is due at school tomorrow and she was struggling with one part, so I wanted to explain it to her before I got carried away with the party."

Lisa loved everything to do with cars and had chosen to do one of her assignments on car engines. Scott had been helping her with it for weeks and I'd decided there wasn't much on this planet better than watching a man helping their child. Although Lisa was not our child, we both treated her as if she was. Her mother had come a long way, and I was confident in her recovery from drug addiction, but we would never stop thinking of Lisa as part of our family.

"I've got it now, so I'm going to go back inside and hang out if that's okay," Lisa said.

"Sure, darlin'," Scott agreed. Jerking his chin towards the restaurant, he added, "Don't let that boy treat you like shit, or I'll be having words with him."

Lisa blushed. "I won't."

I smacked him as we watched her run inside. "Did you have to say that?"

His laughing eyes came to mine, and I sucked in a breath at the crinkles that decorated them. Those damn crinkles. *They get me every time.* "It's her first boyfriend, Harlow, and I'm going to make damn sure she learns straight off the bat that she's entitled to have expectations of being treated a certain way. No boy will ever walk all over her if I have my way."

"Do you know how much I love you, Scott Cole?" I asked as I pressed my body against his.

He took hold of my face and angled my mouth to his. "Almost as much as I love you," he murmured before kissing me again, this time slower and deeper.

My tummy fluttered, just like it always did when he kissed me. I moaned into his mouth. "Baby, I have something to tell you."

He pulled his face away from mine and said, "That you're glad you married me one year ago? That this is the best first anniversary you've ever had?"

"You *are* playful today, aren't you?"

He shrugged. "Life's good, Harlow. Storm's had a year of no huge problems, I've got a beautiful baby daughter, a happy family and a sexy-as-fuck wife whose favourite thing to do is wrap her lips around my dick...I've got all the reasons in the world to smile."

I let his words work their way through my soul, loving how good they felt. And then I whispered, "I've got one more reason for you to smile."

The world around us quietened and slowed as he processed what I said. He stayed silent for what felt like an eternity before finally demanding, "Tell me."

I reached for his hand and placed it on my belly. "You're going to be a daddy again."

His eyes searched mine as his lips slowly spread into the Scott-Cole smile I lived for. "I'm going to be a daddy again," he repeated what I said.

"Yes."

Sliding his arms around me, he pulled me to him again. "This is the best first wedding anniversary I've ever had," he said as his eyes flared with more of the playfulness I could easily get used to.

"Me too, but can I ask you a favour?"

"Depends. How hard is it?"

"Possibly really hard for you."

He chuckled. "Hit me, sweetheart."

"Do you think we could try not to have a repeat of this on our second anniversary?"

"I'm not fuckin' guaranteeing anything. Trying to get you pregnant has become my favourite pastime."

"What do you mean 'trying to get me pregnant'? Have you been plotting this?"

"You didn't realise?"

"No, I just thought it was your love of getting your dick out that was going on. I had no idea it was all part of your life plan."

He placed another kiss on my lips. "Well, I do love getting my dick out, but I also love you being pregnant. Nothing better than seeing my woman with my child in her belly."

"You just loved how big my boobs got." I continued to play with him. This was too much fun.

His eyes dropped to my breasts. "Jesus, how could I forget? Fuck, so many things to look forward to."

I took a deep breath before asking him the one thing I had to know. "So, you're not upset that I'm pregnant again so soon?" I'd discovered my pregnancy a few days ago and had spent that time worrying about telling him. Aurora was only four months old and I'd never expected to get pregnant again so fast.

He tightened his hold on me and his playful mood disappeared. The Scott Cole I knew and loved returned, reminding me why I loved him so much. "Harlow, there

278

isn't a damn thing you could do that would cause me to get upset with you. You're my world, you and Aurora, and any other children we have, and I will always be standing right by your side, holding your hand, and facing whatever we have to face. Together."

"I love you," I said. I had so many words inside that I could say to try and express my love and thankfulness for him, but those three words pretty much covered it all.

He held me and kissed me for a long time. We probably would have stayed there for hours, but Madison interrupted us.

"You two! Everyone's been looking for you guys. I mean, this *is* your party and all," she said while staring at us in exasperation.

I grinned as I stepped out of Scott's embrace. "You're just irritated that you had to get off your chair and come looking for us," I teased her as I rubbed her heavily pregnant stomach. She was due any day now and her cranky mood was at epic levels.

"Fuck you," she muttered and turned to stomp back inside.

Scott placed his arm over my shoulders and we followed her. "It's a shame your Mum isn't here for the party," he said. "Where is she now?"

She'd come home for Aurora's birth and had stayed a few months, but had flown out of the country again two weeks ago. "I Skyped with her this morning, she's in Hawaii, and she's met another man."

279

"Fuck, I hope this one is better than her last one because I'm not fuckin' joking, Harlow...if he breaks her heart, I'll break his goddamn legs."

J met us at the front door of Trilogy as Scott issued his threat of breaking legs. He raised his brows. "Whose legs are we breaking, brother?" he asked.

"Don't encourage him!" Sharon chastised J, but I took in the happy smile on her face. She now held Aurora who reached for her daddy as soon as she saw him come in.

I couldn't hold them in any longer – my tears began falling. They weren't tears of sadness, but rather of happiness. As I stood in the entry to the restaurant and surveyed the room full of our family and friends, I knew deep in my soul that I was beyond blessed.

For all the struggles we'd been through, we'd come out stronger.

We'd fought for love and we'd won.

And life was even better for it.

COMMAND PLAYLIST

Sending a huge shout-out to my Levine's Ladies for their help compiling this playlist!

This Means War – Nickelback
Sad – Maroon 5
Never Tear Us Apart – INXS
Last Request – Paolo Nutini
Locked Away – R. City, Adam Levine
Scars – James Bay
Incomplete – James Bay
Wings – Birdy
Beautiful War – Kings of Leon
Thank You For Loving Me – Bon Jovi
God Gave Me You – Blake Shelton
Bless The Broken Road – Rascal Flatts
Loving You Easy – Zac Brown Band
Love Me Like You Do – Ellie Goulding
Like A Wrecking Ball – Eric Church
All Of Me – John Legend
Breathing – Lifehouse
Hanging By A Moment – Lifehouse
Everything – Lifehouse
Family Tree – Kings of Leon
More Than Words – Extreme

Unbreakable – Jamie Scott

Right Here Waiting – Richard Marx

Trade Hearts – Jason Derulo

Give Me A Sign – Breaking Benjamin

Yours To Hold – Skillet

Broken – Seether, Amy Lee

Recovery – James Arthur

Appreciated – Rixton

Nobody Knows – Pink

Tumble and Fall – Little Big Town

Just Give Me A Reason – Pink. Nate Ruess

Try – Pink

Drag Me Down – One Direction

By The Grace of God – Katy Perry

Waiting For Superman – Daughtry

What's Up – 4 Non Blondes

Brave – Sara Bareilles

Break On Me – Keith Urban

Making Memories of Us – Keith Urban

For You – Keith Urban

ACKNOWLEDGMENTS

To my readers – from the bottom of my heart, thank you for loving my characters as much as I do. Thank you for your friendships. Thank you for your kindness. I truly have the best readers in the world. Command was the last book in this first instalment of the Storm MC Series, but it is definitely not the end of the Storm MC! Havoc's book is up next, and did you see what I did with Wilder? You've gotta know that he's getting a book soon! OH, and what about King? God, I think I want that man for myself... keep an eye out for his book, too. I did plan to write it last in the Sydney Storm MC series, but I've fallen hard for him and I think I'm going to move it up on the list.

To my friend, Jodie – I treasure our friendship so much. I never imagined it to grow how it has, but I'm so very blessed to have you in my life. Thank you for showing me how to be a better friend. Thank you for encouraging me to be the best version of me. Thank you for teaching me that some people can suck my big, hard cock. I really don't think you know just how amazing you are, my friend xx

To my long suffering editor, Karen – thank you for putting up with me... again! Thank you for understanding that sometimes the words just don't come. I truly value your encouragement and support.

To Eric Battershell – thank you for your photo that graces my cover. It is the exact right image for this book and I am in love with it more today than when I bought it. I loved meeting you earlier this year and hope to see you again soon. You have a beautiful soul, Eric – never change for anyone xx

To Letitia, my cover designer – thank you for creating my favourite cover to date! I can't wait to get this book in paperback – I may stare at it for hours!! xx

To my bloggers – thank you for everything you do. Having been a blogger before, I truly do not believe most authors quite understand the dedication you have and the hours you put in. I do, and I am so thankful for it all.

To my girls in Levine's Ladies and Team Levine – I want to acknowledge every single one of you amazing ladies who has taken the time to chat with me, share my books and support me, but honestly, there are so many that I am afraid I will forget some, and in my mind that would be worse than not naming anyone. Please know that if we have chatted in my group or online anywhere, I treasure our friendship. Some people think social media is the devil...I don't, I love what it has given me in some very special friendships.

To Patti West – thank you for contributing the Sex In A Pan recipe for Harlow to make for Scott. And for your beautiful friendship, too. I can't wait to meet you one day, Patti. I adore you – you have a heart of gold and are so kind and giving xx

To my family and friends – thank you for loving me and supporting me as I reach for my dreams. I love you all.

ABOUT THE AUTHOR

Dreamer.
Coffee Lover.
Gypsy at heart.
Bad boy addict.

USA Today Bestselling Aussie author who writes about alpha men & the women they love.

When I'm not creating with words you will find me either creating with paper or curled up with a good book and chocolate.

I love Keith Urban, Maroon 5, Pink, Florida Georgia Line, Bon Jovi, Matchbox 20, Lady Antebellum and pretty much any singer/band that is country or rock.

I'm addicted to Nashville, The Good Wife & wish that they would create a never-ending season of Sons of Anarchy.

Signup for my newsletter: http://eepurl.com/OvJzX

Keep up to date with my books at my website
www.ninalevinebooks.com

Join my fan group on Facebook:
https://www.facebook.com/groups/LevinesLadies/

Facebook: https://www.facebook.com/AuthorNinaLevine
Twitter: https://twitter.com/NinaLWriter
Pinterest: http://www.pinterest.com/ninalevine92/

Also by Nina Levine

USA Today & International Bestselling Author

Storm MC Series

Storm (Storm MC #1)

Fierce (Storm MC #2)

Blaze (Storm MC #3)

Revive (Storm MC #4)

Slay (Storm MC #5)

Sassy Christmas (Storm MC #5.5)

Illusive (Storm MC #6)

Command (Storm MC #7)

Havoc (Storm MC #8) COMING 2016

Sydney Storm MC Series

Relent (Sydney Storm MC #1)

Crave Series

All Your Reasons (Crave #1)

Be The One (Crave #2)

Made in the USA
Monee, IL
02 November 2019

16213647R00164